Meet the New PI in Town, Whether She Likes It or Not
Deb Powers hopes mountain life suits her better.
But an odd case of disappearing tools turns her head.

Something Strange Lurks in a Shadowy World
Deb's cousin brings a case too eerie and weird to ignore.
And an unconventional friend to help Deb see the other side.

Not the Best Place for a Good Night's Sleep
A free stay at a new B&B in town proves too much to resist.
Plus Deb gets a chance to investigate the bizarre house guest.

On the Trail of Something Scary
Eerie incidents spell trouble for all of Estonoa.
Deb takes a chance on digging out the weird.

Echoes of a Plan Gone Wrong
Deb welcomes friends with a neighborly new addition.
But one friend needs her skills to keep her plans on track.

INVESTIGATIONS BEYOND BELIEF

THE INITIAL ADVENTURES OF DEB POWERS: OTHERWORLDLY PI

KARI KILGORE

SPIRAL PUBLISHING, LTD.

CONTENTS

INTRODUCTION

I've long had a fascination with the idea of strange things happening that no one else knows about. I don't mean secretive, logic-defying twist of conspiracy theories, though I understand how a certain type of person can sink into that particular rabbit hole.

I'm talking about that little voice inside that wonders if the folklore, mythology, legends, and even fairy tales we grew up with might have had a grain of truth. Or a whole lot more of a solid basis in reality.

Maybe a reality we've forgotten, or simply turned away from.

I'm quite sure part of my interest in such things began with a life-long love of *The Twilight Zone* and other TV shows, movies, and stories like it. Many of my favorite episodes played right into that idea that of course there are weird things going on around us.

All the time.

It's just that most people don't seem to notice.

Maybe because they're not paying attention, or they're

too "square" or literal-minded to understand what's hiding in plain sight right in front of them.

Maybe because they *do* catch those glimpses and hints and clues. But they work very hard to avoid thinking about what they've seen, heard, or felt. That way they don't have to admit that the world might be a much stranger place than they'd prefer to believe.

Or maybe it's a version of the same impulse that sends people down the endless road of conspiracy theories in the first place. What if only a very few, select, and special people have the ability to see the bizarre nature of the world around us? And they truly are the only ones who know?

Wouldn't it be cool to be one of those rare individuals who have the chance to understand the truth, while everyone else goes about their lives in blissful ignorance?

Sure, that might be cool. Possibly interesting, and even exciting.

But I suspect the "gift" of being one of those people would actually come with a pretty heavy cost.

Being the only one would also carry the potential of other people thinking you're more than a little bit nuts.

And the even greater risk of being alone with that knowledge eventually eroding your mental state, until those other people are proven right after all.

That idea of the fantastic turning out to be reality has played a big part of a lot of my fiction, as it does for many other fantasy writers.

The stories in *Investigations Beyond Belief* aren't only fantasies, even though those elements certainly help shape the stories.

While I was spinning the yarns for this collection, I was also playing with two of my other favorite storytelling tropes: private investigators, and my native Appalachian Mountains.

When it comes to writing and reading mystery and crime

fiction, I'm often drawn to amateur sleuths. These are folks who feel like they wander into the world that doesn't make sense. Not quite like *The Twilight Zone*, with the emphasis on speculative elements.

Amateur sleuths get caught up in crimes of some kind. Sometimes firmly set in the real world, like in *Shadows Mountain Deep*, the anthology my husband Jason A. Adams and I recently published. The characters only *feel* like they've wandered into an alternate reality.

Of course you'll often find amateur sleuths in fantasy or science fiction as well.

But a private investigator is another sort of person—and character. The PI is a professional. This is what they do for a living. They're not generally wandering unsuspecting into a crime, though of course that certainly can happen in their line of work.

Private investigators are sought out and hired, and often licensed and trained in a surprising variety of technology, techniques, and methodologies.

That brings me to Deb Powers, the main character in all the stories from *Investigations Beyond Belief.* Deb has years of experience as a PI, working in the big city of Atlanta. And those years caught up in the rush and busyness of both the city and her line of work have taken their toll.

Deb is ready to move on, from both her work and Atlanta.

She finds herself returning to her family's home in the Appalachian Mountains of Virginia, the setting for so many of my fantasy, crime, and romance stories.

One of the many things that made writing Deb so much fun for me was drawing from my own life. Like Deb, I grew up mostly in the Midwest, with frequent family visits to Virginia. And like Deb, after several years living in Atlanta, life in the fast lane of city life sent me home to the mountains for a slower pace and a major change of scenery.

Part of that decision—moving to where your family is from after years away—is realizing how quickly you lose your anonymity. The ability to simply exist. To succeed or make mistakes in your life without worry about what your family might think.

To live your life without wondering what sort of trouble your family might get you into next.

Deb quickly encounters a first cousin who happens to be the local sheriff. And who also happens to think Deb and the whole community would be much better off with a talented, experienced private investigator among them, still doing the work she's so good at.

To say this cousin brings her most *unusual* cases to Deb would be an understatement.

For me to say more here about those cases would spoil way too much of the fun.

Since another of my favorite genres to read and write is romance, Deb finds herself face-to-face with someone else she frequently spent time with during those childhood visits. Let me just say the old spark and heat between them hasn't entirely died out.

She also finds people she can depend on when it comes to figuring out the huge change in her life. And when it comes to digging into the crimes that seem to defy all the usual crime-solving methods, not to mention the typical understanding of reality.

That's one of the wonderful things about living where we do, with the rich folklore and deep love of tall tales and all sorts of storytelling. Quite a few rituals and routines and beliefs about everyday life have an undercurrent of magic and mystery built right in.

So you might say once Deb showed up in my head, she

made herself at home right away, and in the best way. I expect these five stories will only be the beginning of our adventures together.

I hope you enjoy reading these stories as much as I enjoyed writing them. Check out all kinds of mysterious tales at www.KariKilgore.com/Mystery.

You'll find plenty of stories in almost every genre set in and around my native Appalachian Mountains by paying a visit to www.KariKilgore.com/TalesFromAppalachia.

You can also visit www.KariKilgore.com to learn more about me and find other short stories, along with novellas, novels, and more collections.

Swing by www.ConfidentialAdventureClub.com to keep up with what I'm doing next, get free stories, read exclusive content not available anywhere else, and see adorable pet photos. Hope to see you there!

And last but certainly not least, thank you for your support of me and my writing. It means the world to me and keeps me coming back to tell the next tale.

KARI KILGORE
AUTHOR OF WICKED BONE AND SONGS IN THE MOUNTAIN
DEB POWERS: OTHERWORLDLY PI
MAKING A CHANGE FOR THE STRANGER

For Jason

*Who knows the unusual perspective of being
an insider/outsider as well as I do.*

MAKING A CHANGE FOR THE STRANGER

Most days, Deb Powers loved everything about her new life back home.

She'd set up shop in the cozy walk-out basement in her Great Auntie Zelda's house, giving her a lovely view of the sleepy little town of Estonoa, Virginia, where she and her twin sister Katie spent the first year or so of their lives.

Or at least that's what their parents and truly intimidating swarm of aunts, uncles, and various flavors of cousins had always told them. An embarrassing array of photographs and grainy old VHS videos seemed to back up that claim, though neither Deb nor Katie remembered any of it.

But they did remember coming back to visit the lush mountains and creeks, the secretive valleys and hollers. For holidays or vacations, and for joyful birthdays or heartbreaking funerals.

The place their parents always seemed to miss and long for from the far less wild surroundings of Deb's Cincinnati childhood. The strange northern land her family escaped to, following the irresistible song of more jobs and better opportunities, at least back in those days.

Now Deb couldn't deny an immediate sense of peace, of belonging, every time she looked out across the hilly streets full of low brick buildings and a few white wooden houses. The endless variety of spring green decorating the ring of mountains sheltering Estonoa kept her staring out the basement's row of windows when she really should be working.

She pretended to herself that the next important thing to concentrate on might be...more storage space for her office. She'd brought several sensible black bookshelves with her, and they looked wonderful packed full of books and knick-knacks, set against walls she'd painted a rich cinnamon brown.

Much like her private investigator job back in her adopted-in-adulthood home of Atlanta, Deb didn't expect many walk-in clients in her new career as a computer and technology consultant. But she'd brought in a comfortably overstuffed blue sofa for one wall, and two decidedly *less* comfortable repurposed dining room chairs.

After all, a woman who'd made damn sure she could be her own boss and work from home since she graduated from college wasn't exactly hoping for crowds of people to settle in for a nice, long, neighborly chit-chat.

Same with the decidedly old-fashioned plain wooden desk her Auntie Zelda left behind along with the house. A bit of space between Deb and potential clients was automatically a good thing.

Auntie Zelda left a whole bunch of the books, too, and they covered all kinds of weird and wonderful topics most computer pros (or private investigators) normally wouldn't have out on display.

Deb was starting to wonder about arranging the desk so it faced all those wonderful windows rather than one of the bookshelves, that really were kind of crowded now that she thought about it. Never mind that the books could easily become their own distraction.

Even with two sleek flat-screen monitors and new lightning-fast computer—a splurge from the profits of selling her fabulous in-town Atlanta house—Deb could too easily end up gazing out over the town and the mountains.

Like she was doing right now.

Again.

But who could possibly blame her when the dreamy aroma of early jasmine drifted in through those windows and the screen door, along with the scent of someone nearby with the grill going on this unusually warm early evening?

Or when what she needed to focus on was a marketing plan for her brand-new business? No matter how her mind kept dragging her away in other directions?

Deb sighed, took a sip of the ginger tea she tried to switch to after three p.m. as part of her habitual stress-reduction regimen from her city-living days, and turned (most of) her attention back to planning the backbone of her new life.

The one she'd started clear-headed and with a solid plan.

Not because she was running away. No matter how many different ways her mind tried to convince her of that, along with her perpetually confused twin who still lived in Cincinnati.

Not giving up on a great career, or selling out, or selling herself short.

Simply moving herself away from the high-stress lifestyle that pushed her into such a massive change in the first place.

Just like they had all afternoon, her eyes drifted away from the accusingly blank document on the screen.

This time she had a good reason for the distraction: someone walking up the concrete sidewalk cutting across her backyard. A woman with the same wavy brown hair and blue eyes that Deb, her twin, and so many of the Powers shared, wearing casual blue jeans and a plain black t-shirt.

Deb's mind fell back on her typical PI habit of high-speed cataloging and sorting, but only for a quick second.

That was her cousin Terri Walsh: hard-working sheriff and all-around upstanding citizen. Never mind that Deb clearly remembered what a natural goofball Terri was, and how she utterly adored ghost stories, preferably told outdoors and at night.

Terri grinned as she made a show of knocking on the metal side of the screen door.

"You can see me sitting right here," Deb said, returning the grin. "So just come on in already."

"As an official representative of law enforcement, I really should talk to you about leaving your doors unlocked, ma'am." Terri opened the door and stepped inside, then promptly sprawled on the couch. "You never know who might wander by."

Deb snorted as she got to her feet and stretched, pushing her own wavy brown hair back over her shoulders. She hadn't even made it to Terri's level of presentable today. Her own t-shirt was a rather faded and threadbare gray model she'd gotten for free at some convention years ago, and her sweat-pants weren't any newer. At least all of it was clean.

"You mean besides vagabond cousins looking for a couch to crash on? That I can handle. You don't really expect me to believe there's a dangerous crime wave here in bustling suburban Estonoa, do you?"

Terri stared at her with the same strict, one-eyebrow-raised expression their grandmother used when a scolding was in progress, but it didn't last long. She waved one hand in the general direction of the office.

"Oh yeah, we're really on the mean streets out here. The

place looks great, Deborah. Almost like a grownup works here."

"A grownup who's hated being called Deborah since we were teenagers, *Theresa*. What brings you out here in your civilian getup?"

Deb dodged a predictable elbow jab as she took her place on the couch. At least now that she couldn't look out the window she'd be able to concentrate, or at least she hoped so.

"Okay, *Deb*," Terri said, rolling her eyes. "I partly dropped by just to say hello, believe it or not. I always loved this place growing up. Auntie Zelda would love seeing you do something good with it. Planning to take up your work as a PI again anytime soon?"

"Not even a little bit, you know that. I had my fill of digging into everyone else's business. Time to put some of the hacker-level computer skills I picked up along the way to use. Besides, I'm not even licensed in Virginia, remember?"

Terri's relaxed posture abruptly shifted. She put both feet on the floor and sat forward, elbows on her knees.

Here it comes...

"Yeah, I know that's what you said when you first got here," Terri said. "I was just wondering if you'd had a chance to think it over, maybe. Because we sure do have more cases than you'd expect here that could use a well-trained mind. Especially someone with an insider/outsider perspective."

"Care to tell me what an insider/outsider is?"

Terri shrugged.

"Easy enough. Someone who's plenty familiar with how things work back here in the scary Appalachian Mountains because she grew up with parents from here. Grew up spending almost all her holidays and special occasions here too, even though she lived in a big Midwestern city and moved to a big Southern city. Someone who understands who we are because she's one of us, but she's always been a visitor at the same time."

She shook her head and blew her bangs off her forehead.

"Hell, Deb, you know as well as I do what I mean. You *are* an insider/outsider."

Deb crossed her arms, and she felt her mouth quirking into one of their Auntie Zelda's expressions without her permission. Twisted over to one side in an accurate declaration that she believed whatever had just been stated to be pure, unfiltered horseshit.

"You expect me to go *that* far down the road of speculation and psychobabble with you? Okay then, you've got my attention enough to listen, mainly because I'm looking for an excuse to not work on my marketing plan today. Please *do* explain why you're here telling me all of this."

"Marketing plan, really? Ugh." Terri shuddered, then went on in an exaggerated version of her soft, musical accent. "I reckon you'll be thankin' me right quick for rescuing you from all that fuss and nonsense."

Deb laughed, but her mind was racing far ahead of the conversation, and ahead of the situation she didn't know enough about to have an opinion yet.

What if she really wasn't ready to change every single thing in her life? Maybe leaving her chosen home in Atlanta, selling her beloved in-town bungalow, relocating to a small town in a state she knew well but had never lived in, *and* an abrupt career change on top of the rest was a bit too much.

She shook her head and let out a long sigh instead.

"I don't know, Terri. I loved my work, and here's where you know as well as I do that I was pretty damn good at it. I'm going to guess you also know how exhausting it was, how often I was chasing after heartbreak that was almost as hard for me to deliver as for my clients to hear. I'll listen to you, but I can't make any promises beyond that."

Terri nodded and agreed way too fast for Deb's comfort.

And she had a mischievous glint in her eye that was even less reassuring.

"Well good. Now that we have your token resistance out of the way, here's what I've got. You remember Jeff Denton, one of the kids we hung out with at Granny's house out on Apple Branch? He lived close by, but we hardly ever saw him unless he knew *you* were visiting. Then he was there quick as a flash and wouldn't leave until you did."

Deb was surprised to feel a blush heating her cheeks. Here she was at the ripe old age of forty-two, veteran and survivor of more relationships than she cared to think about right now, including a long one that ended in the breakup that helped lead to her move.

And she still got a goofy-little-kid thrill thinking about things that happened thirty years ago.

"Yeah, I remember Jeff. Cute kid, skinny as a rail, curly red hair and a mess of freckles. I haven't seen or heard of him for ages. Does he still live around here?"

Terri winked, and Deb suppressed an urge to kick her out and do whatever it took to put a restraining order in place to keep her from coming back. Which made perfect sense since Terri was the sheriff, and annoyance didn't exactly justify restraining orders.

Even though she sometimes thought it should.

"The good news here is Jeff moved back himself about a year ago. He joined up with the Air Force right out of high school, got his college degree while he was in, and went on to technical writing school. Turns out his job was more than happy to pay him the same money and let him work from his house, so he took it one step farther and moved back home."

"Okay, I'll ask and probably regret it later. What's the bad news?"

This time Terri at least frowned instead of looking smug.

"Jeff moved into the house next door to his dad Wayne, who you may or may not remember has always been a good ways past peculiar. Right down from Granny and Poppa's house, same as always. Wayne's not a bad guy by any means, and no one could deny he's actually one of the smartest people around. But he's got what you might call a unique outlook on life. Anyway, seems things have developed a habit of going missing around Wayne's place over the last several years, but he never told anybody until Jeff came back."

"And then Jeff reported it to you. I'm guessing you're *not* telling me this because you solved the case. What's the rest of it?"

Now Terri turned sideways on the couch to face Deb again, crossing her own arms.

"The rest of it is we can't find the first clue about what might be going on. Part of the trouble is it's mostly small stuff. He has that big garage stuffed full, but it's all as organized as can be. One of his strange habits is he takes pictures of things, always has. Files them away—for insurance purposes he says—even though he retakes the same ones about once a month. *And* he compares them. That's how he noticed the trouble. A screwdriver here, a tape measure there. A few nails or nuts and bolts. Bits of wire and even the old-clothes-rags he keeps for wiping up spills."

"That's worth reporting? Sounds to me like Wayne's doing pretty good if that's the only trouble he's having, Terri."

"I know, I know. That's what I thought at first when Jeff called. But he and Wayne started adding things up, and it's a lot when you put it together. That and things have started disappearing from *inside* Wayne's house now. Slices of bread, the odd sock. A fork, a pack of sewing needles. A bunch of matches and several ink pens. It just doesn't make sense."

Deb scowled, all at once convinced this was nothing more than a convoluted scheme to get her to spend time with Jeff after all these years. Not that she would especially object to *seeing* him, mind you, but this was just weird enough to be off-putting.

"Security cameras?" she said. "Checking for fingerprints? And I hate to say this, but you'd be surprised how often things like this happen with families and it's not any kind of crime. Maybe see how Wayne's doing as far as forgetfulness? I know one family was certain grandma's coin collection was getting carried off by the grandkids, but it turned out grandpa was putting them in a hiding place in the closet all along, to keep them safe. But he honestly couldn't remember doing that."

Terri raised one hand and held it flat against the window screen, where the setting sun was finally hiding all the distractions.

"Jeff started taking Wayne to all of his doctor's appointments when he came back, and not because Wayne was having memory trouble. He's having trouble seeing at night is all. No signs of mental decline so far. We searched Wayne's place top to bottom, everywhere he had photos of things missing. Not a trace of fingerprints or footprints or anything else. Here's the part that really got my attention, even though it didn't help."

She stopped, bringing her hand down and lacing her fingers together in her lap. She stared down at them instead of looking at Deb.

"Now listen, this is going to sound out there, I know. I can hear the words inside my head before I say them, but that doesn't change a thing. I'm asking you to hear me out before you decide *I'm* the one off my rocker. Think you can do that?"

Terri looked into Deb's eyes then, and Deb didn't see a hint of teasing or joking. In fact, Terri seemed nervous of all things. As if she was worried about what Deb might think of her.

"Come on, Terri, you know me better than that. Mainly because I've known you all our lives. I don't doubt for one second that you know the difference between tall tales and your work. And my work, back when it was my work. I'm not about to judge you, okay?"

Terri took a deep breath and let it out even slower.

"Okay. This is between you and me. Or between you and me, and Jeff and Wayne, because they showed me. Jeff is another nerdy type like you are, to be honest. When Wayne first told him all of this, Jeff set up security cameras all around the place. Everywhere things disappeared. They worked perfectly, for a while. And for a while, everything stayed put. Then the cameras shorted out, pretty much one at a time."

Deb hated like fire to admit it, but her curiosity was up and excited. The same deep drive to know, to understand, to figure it out, that had gotten her into PI work in the first place.

Along with a little tickle of the same breathless sense of wonder that had her telling ghost stories outside under the stars right alongside Terri all those years ago. Sometimes right here in this same backyard, with Auntie Zelda joining them, and as giggly and shivery as the kids were.

More often out in the relative wilderness of their grandparents' house.

Generally with cute and funny and very attentive Jeff Denton close by.

"I'll ask the obvious questions," she said. "Even though I have an idea you and Jeff already covered all of this. Any pattern to the cameras going out, like maybe they were a bad batch? Maybe wiring trouble in the house? And I guess the real question is, did things start disappearing again when the cameras failed?"

Terri grinned, leaned forward, and grabbed Deb's hand for a quick second.

"I *knew* you were the right one to talk to about all of this. Jeff showed me the time stamps on the camera footage, and neither of us could find reason or rhyme to when they failed. It seemed random as far as when and where they died, and they were totally shorted out, like someone hit them with too much voltage. Just a flash, and out. He had an electrician in to check the wiring, which was all good. And yes indeed, the one and only pattern we did find was soon as the cameras went dark, stuff went missing in that spot again."

Deb shook her head and stared up at the ancient dropped ceiling, made up of old-school papery white tiles with tiny little black dots everywhere. One of the many lingering signs of her Auntie Zelda that she liked too much to rip out and replace.

"That *is* more than a little strange. I'm still not committing to anything, but what are you thinking? Want me to head over and check it out? Talk to Jeff and his dad?"

Terri blushed bright red, and Deb knew the truly big ask was about to step out into the open at last.

"Sure, that makes sense. But that really would be going back over ground we already covered. Trouble is we have so *much* ground to cover in the whole county that we're short-handed most of the time. On top of that, I don't have anyone trained to do what you do. And yes, I do know you're damn good at it."

"Enough flattery, Sheriff Walsh. Cousin or not, cut it and get to the point. There have to be private investigators around here I'm sure. Detectives, too."

Terri held both hands up.

"Absolutely, and fine investigators they are. They'd be none too happy with me if they knew I wanted to bring you in instead. But the truth is there's something strange here, Deb. I *feel* it, I know it in my bones. I don't trust anyone besides you to handle this one."

Deb rubbed her mouth and chin, gazing out at the darkening sky, with streaks of pink cutting through the blue. Someone else was grilling now, and she heard kids playing somewhere nearby as the streetlights popped on.

"All right, Terri. You've got me hooked for this one. But don't count on any others, hear me? Again, I'm not licensed in Virginia, and I don't plan to be. Not that I expect to get into anything all that cloak and dagger on this case. When do you want to get started?"

The office was starting to get a little too dim for doing much, but it was plenty clear enough to see Terri trying (and failing) to keep from smiling.

"You still as much of a night owl as when we were kids?"

Deb laughed, reluctantly letting herself move all the way from suspicious to curious.

And admitting that little churn in her belly was more excitement than nerves.

"Why do you think I was finally getting started on that blasted marketing plan when almost everyone else is getting home from work? That's one of the many reasons I've always been better off working for myself. Spill it."

"I thought so," Terri said, nodding and smiling. "I manage to keep myself forced into a daytime schedule, but I snap back to the moonlight shift any time I have more than a couple of days off. Interested in an old-school stakeout? I have the feeling it's going to take human eyes to catch whatever's going on at Wayne's place."

"With Jeff along as an accomplice, right?" When Terri shrugged, Deb again fought the urge to kick her out. But she didn't have to fight it all that hard this time. "You going to pretend this has nothing to do with the way he used to carry on about me? Assuming he's not married."

Terri got to her feet in one easy motion and held out a hand, which Deb made a point of refusing.

"He *was* married, sure. But he moved back home by himself. I never did hear a reliable rumor about why that was. I wouldn't mind a bit to see either one of you have a little fun, no. But this really is because I know you'll take me seriously. And because I trust you."

Deb walked over to her desk and turned on a black adjustable lamp that looked just enough like a strange metallic insect lurking to make her happy.

"I guess that will have to do. What time do you think, eleven o'clock? Midnight?"

"How about this?" Terri said. "I'll get in touch with Jeff and ask what he thinks with his Dad's schedule. I'm sure you remember where it is. I think midnight makes sense, but this is between you two. Join me for dinner down at the brewery?"

Deb shook her head, already thinking through what she'd need for the job.

First thing needed to be ditching the ginger tea for a good, strong cup of coffee. Next would be getting another look a few of the stranger volumes among Auntie Zelda's books.

"Naaaah, maybe next time. Got some work to do before I can get to work. I remember exactly where it is. I'm guessing you won't be joining us on the overnight?"

"Nope, but I honestly wish I could. I'm up at the ass-crack of dawn tomorrow." Terri stopped, one hand on the door. "Thank you, Deb, truly. I appreciate this more than you know."

"We'll see about that once this is all said and done and you get my bill."

"You bet, and no family discount rate, either. I know you're worth every last penny."

DEB'S HANDS only did a little bit of the caffeine jitter when she stepped out of her car at Wayne Denton's place about ten minutes before midnight.

The tiny cluster of houses didn't look any different than she remembered by her headlights or the faint light of the half-moon. Two on one side of the winding ridge-top road, one on the other. All of them standard two-story with white wood siding, small yards in front and back, and big family-size garden plots.

The huge matching garage that was apparently the start of all the strangeness sat between the two houses on this side, only one story tall but wide enough to hold three cars and deep enough for that many more if Deb remembered right.

No lights on in any of them, but everything was too neatly kept for even her vivid imagination to convince her that they were really abandoned and this was nothing but a horrible joke.

Beyond the tiny Denton settlement, the rest of the road had trees thick and close on both sides. A family and homey island surrounded by mountain wilderness: hardly any more tame than it had been a hundred years before.

Dark and mysterious, and much noisier than Deb's neighborhood back in Atlanta, with peepers and frogs singing their springtime mating songs. The night had cooled quite a bit once the sun went down, but she hadn't brought anything other than a black hoodie to go with her typical nighttime uniform of a charcoal-gray long-sleeved shirt and jeans.

She smelled the creek running close by that provided the froggy love nests, along with a faint scent of freshly turned earth in at least one of those garden plots.

The reason for the rest of her jitters stepped onto the front porch of the house next door, into a circle of faint reddish light that was surely meant to preserve night vision.

Even if Deb didn't know Jeff lived there, she would have recognized him at first sight.

He stood only a little taller than she did, and he wore a muted flannel shirt to go with his own jeans. His porch light was plenty bright enough to show how remarkably kind the years had been to him.

Jeff walked toward her, brushing one hand over his not-quite-long curly hair, then smoothing his one-step-away-from-shaggy beard. He'd filled out nicely too, with strong shoulders and only a comfortable hint of extra padding around his middle.

She didn't need brighter light to remember how bright his green eyes were.

His smile had only gotten more charming, which Deb didn't think was possible.

"Hey Deborah, great to see you again."

His smooth, resonant voice and warm handshake were almost enough to make up for the throwback thing with her name.

"Hey Jeff, great to see you too. It's Deb these days."

He touched his forehead and frowned, and didn't look any less handsome.

"That's *right*, Terri told me that just a few hours ago. I'll do my best not to slip up, but don't hesitate to remind me." He glanced toward his father's house, still entirely dark. "I won't waste your time right now, but I'd love to catch up now that we're both back in town."

Through her automatic focus on the job at hand, Deb was surprised at how much she wanted to do the same thing.

"Sure, that sounds great to me. And long overdue. So, Terri told me about stuff going missing, and the security cameras taking themselves out. Anything else strange I need to know about before we get started?"

He brushed his hair back again, and Deb might get annoyed with herself about it later, but she couldn't help noticing he wasn't wearing a wedding ring.

"You mean this-whole-situation strange? Or more like I'm-not-sure-I-should-admit-this-to-anyone strange?"

The same eerie prickling up her spine that had Deb packing up several of Auntie Zelda's books in the car rippled through her again.

"Tell me anything that's got you paying attention to it. I'm sure you remember all the creepy stories we used to scare each other with, so don't worry about me thinking you're off the deep end."

Jeff laughed quiet and deep, and that got more of Deb's attention from head to toe than she wanted to admit.

"I've been wondering if me and Dad both aren't getting closer to that deep end lately. Besides what Terri told you, the odd thing to me is Dad's not even a little bit upset about any of this. Honestly, he seems to think it's kind of...*funny* almost. Like it's all a big adventure. Which I guess it kind of is, since no one's getting hurt and nothing all that valuable is disappearing at once."

He put his hands on his hips and looked toward the dark and silent garage.

"I'd chalk it up to simple forgetfulness if it wasn't for that thing with the cameras."

Deb looked closer herself, now that her eyes were adjusting after her drive. She spotted two tiny red lights—no, four of them—around the edges of the closed garage doors.

"Yeah, that's unusual," she said. "I was thinking I should set up near one of them tonight. Any chance a camera or two shorted out recently?"

Jeff nodded, and she could see his wonderful big smile better, too.

"Yep, right inside the garage door closest to Dad's house, just last night. I replaced one of them, but I haven't plugged it in yet. Maybe I could do that, then bring us out something warm to drink and snack on?"

Deb returned his smile before her mouth could get into gear and ruin everything.

"I'd normally say I work alone, and that's the only thing my insurance will cover. But since this isn't an official job and I wouldn't mind the company, that all sounds good to me."

Jeff rubbed his hands together, a goofy, kind of endearing habit he'd had all those years ago.

"Great, I'll open that door and run back inside and grab the stuff. I mixed up half-decaf, half-regular for myself. That work for you?"

"You bet, that sounds just right." She decided not to tell him she had exactly the same thing packed in an old-school green metal thermos in her car's back seat. "I'll grab the night-vision goggles. Lucky for you I always travel with a spare. Will Wayne be joining us?"

Jeff shook his head with a sad smile as they walked toward the garage.

"He's turned into quite the early-to-bed type over the last few years, so no. I doubt he'll hear anything that happens out here short of a whole wall of his tools falling over. But he was pretty excited about someone coming to check it out."

He rolled the door up by hand instead of with a remote, and right away Deb spotted more of the camera lights. Jeff had installed them in a good configuration: about every six feet and about the same height from the concrete floor she could make out by the dim moonlight. The rest of the garage was dark.

And going by the pattern, two of the tiny red lights were missing, side by side.

"I'll get the goggles and meet you back here," Deb said.

A couple of minutes later she stood in the same spot, heavy goggles on and activated. Getting a look at what had to be the most organized garage she'd ever seen in her life under an otherworldly greenish glow.

The whole three-car space was open, with only a pickup truck that looked a well-kept ten years old or so in the middle space. The rest was lined with waist-high wooden workbenches, sets of metal drawers on wheels, and a vast expanse of pegboard.

All manner of tools hung from hooks or rested on shelves or fit onto clever little holders set into the pegboard, with shelves full of books and manuals tucked in between. Deb noticed several empty spaces in the tools, along with several more on a wall covered with neat bundles of various kinds of wire and clever little bins full of screws and nails and nuts and bolts.

A couple of the kind of outdoor chairs that folded up into a straight, portable bundle sat beside the pickup truck, facing the wall with the missing security lights. One of the cameras did have a little black cable hanging loose underneath.

Sure, the clean concrete floor had dark stains here and there, and the place had the oil and gas and tire and general vehicle aroma of a garage. But Deb doubted any of the motorheads in her family had a space anywhere near this clean and tidy.

She turned at soft footsteps behind her, and Jeff walked in carrying an old-fashioned wooden picnic basket. He set it down between the two chairs and shrugged.

"It was the only thing I could find. I've got the coffee, grapes, chips, and string cheese. A few molasses cookies. Not a feast, I know, but I figured it's the least I could do."

Deb smiled and handed him her spare goggles. Not quite as heavy as the ones she wore, and not quite as high-resolution. But every bit as bug-eyed and goofy looking.

"I usually subsist on coffee that will etch your teeth and stale vending machine junk if I don't plan ahead and bring it myself. Thank you, Jeff."

He ducked his head and smiled, and Deb had the uncanny sensation of rocketing back in time.

They weren't in their forties, back home after the surprising twists and turns of life, along with possibly more than the usual number of bruises.

They were seven, nine, eleven years old, sitting on blankets or old towels on the dew-damp ground, surrounded by cousins and friends and a million fireflies.

Giggling and shivering at the bizarre tales that flew as fast and thick as the broad expanse of stars overhead.

"You're quite welcome, Deb. I promise I won't chatter and distract you while you're working. Help me get these things turned on, and we'll see what happens."

After a couple of quick adjustments and a gasp of wonder when he saw the garage under the electronic green glow, Jeff plugged in the replacement security camera.

And he was as good as his word once they settled into the not-quite-comfortable chairs. Much to her surprise—and annoyance when she remembered her dear cousin Terri's wink—Deb *really* wanted to get caught up with Jeff now rather than waiting.

Before she worked up the nerve and lack of professionalism to suggest it, motion just outside the garage door caught her eye.

Something that seemed to flutter and dance.

Several somethings.

First near ground level, then higher. Floating around the threshold of the door.

Following one of the gut-level suspicions that made her so good in her former line of work, Deb reached up as slowly as she could manage and flipped the goggles off.

The green glow faded from her vision.

But the dancing objects took on the same hue and light.

She started to lean over and whisper in Jeff's ear, pointing out their firefly visitors.

Then she froze.

Her memories of fireflies didn't match up with the chill in the springtime air around them, even inside the garage.

No, those were summertime critters.

Suited for warm, muggy nights when no one had to be up for school (or work) in the morning.

She jumped at a hand on her arm, and goosebumps chased down her arms at warm breath in a soft whisper against her ear.

"Do you see those lights?"

She started to whisper in turn, but the lights gathered in a knot right outside the door, then rushed inside together.

Not toward the two of them, like she more than halfway expected.

But in a straight line toward the security camera Jeff had plugged in not that long ago.

He squeezed her arm, so she guessed he'd seen it too.

She heard him gasp at a low sizzle, as the hairs on her arms and the back of her neck rose.

A blinding *flash*...

Deb blinked furiously, and by the time her vision cleared, the flying green lights were gone.

Along with the camera's red light.

Powering her goggles back up revealed one of the set of narrow woodworking chisels that had been hanging below it was missing too.

"Did you see *that?*" she whispered, only then realizing she'd grabbed Jeff's hand.

"I saw *something*." He sounded as breathless as she felt. "But I'm not about to guess at what."

"Listen, is there some kind of...I don't know, kind of a cave or a hollow or maybe where an animal could make a den nearby? I know it sounds nuts, but it's something I read in one of my Auntie Zelda's books before I came out here tonight."

She barely managed not to laugh at how downright alien he looked, tilting his head with big, rounded lenses instead of eyes.

"There's a bunch of places where the dirt slumps down by the creek, around the roots of trees. Behind the house. What could you *possibly* be thinking we saw just now?"

Deb squeezed his hand and reluctantly let go.

"Come on, let's go check it out first. Then I'll tell you even if we don't find anything at all."

She grabbed one of her palm-sized metal flashlights and stood, delighted when Jeff stood right beside her.

"These goggles are wild. Come on, it's right this way."

Outside the garage, the night exploded into life, with the stars and the moon overhead lending just enough light to accentuate everything around them in green. The trimmed grass lawn out back only went about thirty feet before the land gave over to brush and trees, and dropped off toward the water and all those singing frogs.

Jeff led the way to a clear path, through the trees and then to obviously human-made steps down to the water. The creek ran high and cheerful, splashing over rocks and going still in little pools off to the side.

The frogs fell silent even with both of them walking carefully and quietly, leaving only the music of the water.

Once they reached the flat, grassy sliver of ground at the bottom, Deb removed her goggles and motioned for Jeff to do the same.

For a few seconds, she couldn't have seen her own hand in front of her face.

Then she caught a faint green glow out of the corner of her eye.

She stepped close to Jeff and leaned up to whisper in his ear, resolving to ignore the enticing scent of his hair and skin.

"Are those slumps off to the left?"

She felt him nod and turn that way, then he fumbled and gripped her hand, warm and tight.

"You see that, don't you? That glow?"

"I do. I'm going to crawl up close to it for a better look."

Jeff drew her hand close against his side, and she felt how fast he was breathing.

Almost as fast as she was.

"You think it's safe?" he whispered. "Whatever you read about in your Auntie Zelda's book?"

Deb fought back a giggle. Less than six hours ago, she couldn't have imagined anything remotely like this happening to her.

But more than thirty-five years ago, on any number of those endless summer nights, she never would have doubted either the eerie glow or Jeff by her side for a second.

"I believe so, yeah. It feels safe, don't you think?"

"I believe so too," Jeff whispered.

She was startled at how cold the grass was against her hands, and her knees were damp right away as they crawled forward. By now her eyes were adjusted enough that she saw the glow from a bunch of spots up ahead. Like looking at a miniature sports arena, maybe, or a tiny spaceship powered down for the night.

The two of them scooted forward on their bellies for the last couple of feet, aiming for one of the bigger openings.

Shoulder to shoulder, Deb and Jeff looked inside.

And both of them forgot how to breathe.

A swarm of tiny figures moved around inside what looked like a rounded sort of natural warehouse, and every last one of them projected their own source of that greenish firefly light.

Miniscule women and men, only a few inches high, dressed in what Deb guessed would be dark brown and green. Maybe even made of leaves and tree bark for all she knew.

The glow came from their exposed skin.

They moved through and around a carefully arranged hoard of what looked like all the missing things from the garage. Stacked against the dirt and tree root walls. Hanging from some of the higher loops and knots of wood. Piled on the smoothed dirt floor.

Deb spotted metal and fabric and wire, and the recently taken chisel right in the center of it all. One of the extremely small people buffed the metal end, while another rubbed the wooden handle with a bit of cloth no bigger than the end of a thumbtack.

She held her breath for several seconds, wondering what she should possibly say or do, if anything. She settled for a whisper to make sure she didn't scare them too badly or hurt their miniscule ears.

"Hello?"

All the activity in the little den stopped. The creatures inside slowly turned until every tiny eye focused on Deb.

This time the goosebumps all over her body felt like ants making tracks across her skin.

She swallowed through a sandpaper throat and decided she'd already brought her mind and her body this far. Might as well try one more step.

"Can you understand me?"

Every miniature head shook back and forth for a second.

Then they all winked out of sight at once, plunging the mysterious warehouse into darkness.

Without a word between them, Deb and Jeff crawled backward. When they were about ten feet away, the green glow popped back into life, along with the impression of movement.

They kept up the slow retreat, getting to their feet when the ground underneath squished with creek water. They stayed quiet on the way back to the garage.

Once they got there, Jeff pulled a squat candle out of his picnic basket and lit it.

Both of them collapsed into chairs that creaked in protest.

"What..." he breathed. "I have no idea where I was going with that thought. What do we do now?"

Deb shook her head, trying to get her own whirling thoughts to slow. It worked about as well as her wish that her heart would let off the gas a little now that they were somewhere that more or less made sense.

"All I can tell you is what I read in Auntie Zelda's book. Those didn't quite seem to be faeries. Or pixies. Or anything else, exactly. But they seemed a lot like several of those kinds of creatures."

"You mean the ones our ancestors believed in?" Jeff said, leaning toward her. "Hundreds or thousands of years ago?"

"I guess that's just what I mean. Maybe these came with them when they crossed the ocean to get here? It wasn't only people from Wales or Scotland or Ireland or England who had legends like this. There are tales of little people from all over the world. Maybe these were here to begin with. Anyway, most of the time, when humans make them mad, they expect some kind of offering rather than a couple of clumsy humans trying to crash onto their turf, demanding explanations. Not like blood or anything, at least I hope not."

Jeff leaned toward the basket and pulled out a bundle wrapped in paper towels.

"And we have no idea if Dad made them angry when all this started, but it's a good bet we did just now. So it's probably a good thing we got ourselves out of there in a hurry. An offering, huh? You mean like food. Like these molasses cookies."

Deb grinned, feeling even more like that pre-teen kid.

"Let's try it. We'll take some down there, and leave the rest around the garage. Then call it a night and see what happens. But only if you promise to call me first thing and tell me what you find when you get up."

Jeff caught her hand one more time.

"Believe me, you'll hear from me again, and before another thirty years go by. I promise. Assuming I ever manage to get to sleep myself."

THE NEXT MORNING (AFTERNOON, technically), Deb grabbed her phone before she even blinked the sleep out of her eyes.

Her heart skipped a beat at the first message on the screen.

Cookies all gone. One perfectly cleaned and polished screwdriver on the garage floor. Dad happy but VERY curious. Meet me for brunch in town?

She sat up, giggling so hard she could barely manage to type.

Forget it, my friend. I'll meet you at the garage in an hour. And I'm bringing the cookies this time!

KARI KILGORE
AUTHOR OF WICKED BONE AND SONGS IN THE MOUNTAIN
DEB POWERS: OTHERWORLDLY PI
A CAVE OF WHISPERING SECRETS

*For everyone tempted by the mystery
of a wild cave*

A CAVE OF WHISPERING
SECRETS

COMPARED to the sodden heat and humidity of Atlanta long before summer settled in, a springtime rainstorm in the Appalachian Mountains was pure paradise.

Deb Powers was glad pretty much every day that she'd made the big move out of the big city. But sitting on the comfy blue sofa in her basement home office, bundled up in one of the countless afghans her Auntie Zelda made years ago, and watching the rain turned this into her new favorite day in a hurry.

She could still see the ring of mountains that surrounded Estonoa through the steady downpour, and the muted green of the thick trees drinking in all that rain. The mostly red brick buildings of the hilly town below her were visible too, with hardly any people or cars out on this lovely Saturday afternoon.

The addition of ghostly streamers and wisps of fog drifting across the view under the gray sky turned the beautiful scene into a relaxing and somehow eerie vista.

The air was still warm enough outside to let her have the big basement windows open, and the purple and green afghan combined with her favorite old sweatpants, a fairly new t-shirt with a nerdy joke about hexadecimal color codes, and a goofy peach hoodie kept her nice and toasty.

The fresh smell and occasional misty breeze added to the sensory delight she couldn't get enough of.

Unlike the marketing plan for her new computer consulting business, currently open on the laptop perched on her knees.

Which was honestly not much more than a blank document with columns for things she *should* be adding to it.

Action items would be the term if she recalled correctly from listening to her friends who worked in Corporate America back in Atlanta, and from her twin sister Katie who did the same in Cincinnati. The idea of competitive addition and subtraction of a never-ending list of *action items* was one of the things that chased Deb into working for herself straight out of college.

She reached for the raspberry tea on the slate gray rug beside her, surprised that the black mug with "Virginia Is for Lovers" across the front had gone cold. She'd been sitting there with her laptop for longer than she thought.

Thankfully one of the tea's virtues—besides letting her aspire to getting to sleep at a so-called reasonable hour—was it didn't get foul and bitter like cold coffee did.

Deb finished the tea, savoring the thin coat of honey collected at the bottom. One of her many nearby cousins had several beehives and was happy to share.

A rumble of thunder surprised her into looking out the window just in time to see a figure turn up the sidewalk cutting through her soggy back yard, huddled under an enormous bright yellow umbrella. Whoever the extremely rare client was (probably because Deb hadn't exactly opened her new business yet), they wore hiking boots, jeans, and a red and blue flannel shirt.

Given what she'd seen of Estonoa's fashion trends when she visited family over the years, that outfit meant practically anyone in the county could be stopping by for a visit.

But she had a suspicion who it would be before the mystery person tilted the umbrella back and proved her right.

Her first cousin Terri Walsh. Sheriff around these parts, and the only one who seemed bound and damned determined that Deb should resume her former life as a private investigator. Never mind that Deb had left that career behind as surely as she left Atlanta and her last long-term relationship.

With no intention of going back to any of them.

On the other hand, the case Terri had talked Deb into a couple of weeks ago had been a few light years away from ordinary. If you could possibly call the discovery of some kind of odd Appalachian tool-stealing (and cleaning) faeries anything short of shocking.

Almost as shocking as Deb spending a good bit of time with an old friend since that mind-altering night. A friend with the potential to turn into a whole lot more.

She pushed the afghan to the back of the sofa and got up to let Terri in, with a half-hearted wish that a new case and not-at-all-subtle encouragement to take up the old line of work wouldn't come in along with her.

After all the wonder and excitement of that first case, though, combined with the quiet thrill of a possible new romance, Deb didn't wish the potential new investigation away all that hard.

Terri stopped under the tiny roof and miniature porch— a concrete pad with barely enough room for two people and one angular blue Adirondack chair Deb hadn't used yet. If she actually sat outside, not only would she get even less of her computer consulting work done, but she feared visitors would turn into a non-stop and even worse distraction.

"You could expand this space a little," Terri said, shaking her umbrella out and leaning it against the freshly painted white cinderblock basement wall. "Maybe have enough room for people to sit and visit from time to time."

"I've got a porch upstairs for that, which I'm sure you remember just fine. Besides, you're the only one who insists on dropping by unannounced."

Terri grinned as she walked past Deb and flopped on the couch, immediately claiming the purple and green afghan and draping it over her legs.

"I don't believe I'm the only one for one hot second. You expect me to believe Jeff hasn't been over here at all since you two hooked up?"

Deb rolled her eyes, then turned away to hide her blush. She had the perfect excuse in opening the micro-closet that she'd hacked out from the already small basement when she did a little move-in remodeling. Besides that, painting the walls a luscious cinnamon brown, and installing a ton of black bookshelves that were already stuffed full, the place had suited her from day one.

She turned back with another afghan, this one a lovely autumnal orange and green, then wrapped it around her shoulders and joined Terri on the couch.

"Jeff and I didn't *hook up*, as you so crudely put it. I helped him and his father with their little theft problem is all. I've seen Jeff a few times since, sure. Mainly to keep working on the case *you* sent me on. Thanks for the generous check, by the way."

Terri gave a half-assed two-finger salute.

"You're quite welcome, from the county and from my personal discretionary fund. Part of me can't believe I'm actually asking you this, but have you and your new man made any progress on...I don't know, getting in touch with the teeny little thieves?"

Deb kicked Terri's leg, *somewhat* gently.

"My *friend* Jeff and his father and I haven't done much more than leave out food for the mountain faeries, or pixies or whatever they are. What we've learned is they're partial to sweets. Any time we leave out cookies or candy or even something like a slice of pie, they take it and leave one of the tools they swiped in its place the next morning."

Terri laughed, shaking her head. She had the same wavy brown hair as Deb, and the typical Powers blue eyes. Unlike Deb, who struggled to get her hair to do anything besides exactly what it wanted to, especially on a rainy day like this, Terri's looked more or less on purpose most of the time.

"What do they do if you leave something else? Like a cracker or, I don't know, a chicken leg?"

"So far, they just take the food and don't bring back anything. To tell you the truth, I'm kind of afraid to try meat with them. They may only be a few inches tall, but there are quite a few of them. And from the kinds of things they were stealing from the garage and inside the house, no human door, lock, or security camera can keep them out."

"I can imagine it now." Terri shuddered. "Swarms of little bitty glowing people, dressed in brown and green like the trees, sneaking in to gnaw on your fingers and toes in the middle of the night, all while armed with the tools and kitchen stuff they scampered away with. *That* would have been a great story for telling around the fire when we were kids."

"Great for nightmare fuel, you mean. And for never setting foot outdoors after the sun goes down, even though you'd never sleep another wink. I'm afraid to ask, but is there any chance this is nothing more than one of your charming social visits?"

Eyes wide and mouth open in shock, Terri held one hand to her chest.

"I can't *believe* you would think such things of me, Deborah. After all the happy hours we spent together in this very house, getting spoiled rotten by Auntie Zelda. Who would be properly horrified by not only your question, but your shocking oversight in not offering me anything to drink or eat. You'd think I'd rate higher than a bunch of critters that could take a bath in your coffee cup there."

"Uh-huh, tell me another one," Deb said. "How about this. You tell me why you're here, Theresa, and I'll decide from there what kind of drink I'll offer. I'll warn you the tap water can be a wee bit over-chlorinated in town this time of month."

"Don't I know it." Terri wrinkled her nose. "The ladies' at the courthouse smelled like a swimming pool yesterday. Maybe I'll pass on the beverage, but I *am* here for more than a social call. You think any more about getting yourself licensed for PI work here in Virginia?"

Deb took a slow breath, focusing on one of the intricate wool knots in her auntie's afghan.

She had been thinking about that. A lot. Especially since she'd made almost exactly zero progress in setting up her new business despite a constant running commentary in her mind reminding her she needed to.

An inherited house combined with a fantastic sale price for her Atlanta house would keep her going for a good long while if she was careful.

But not forever.

Not to mention the lurking twin demons of boredom and feeling like she was wasting time, except for the more-wonderful-than-she-wanted-to-admit time spent with Jeff.

"I don't know, Terri," she fibbed, not very effectively going by the way Terri's eyes lit up. "I'll probably regret this, but I'll listen to what you have to say."

"No ma'am, you won't regret it for one second." Terri

turned sideways on the couch. "Because this one is right up your bizarre little investigative alley. You remember the cave under the high school?"

"Not sure I could forget the place where you almost got me suspended the summer before our senior year, and I didn't even go to school here."

This time Terri shoved at Deb's leg with her booted foot.

"Just can't stop accusing me, can you? Not my fault you managed to get yourself caught by falling into that mud puddle. I was the one who had to play the perfect angel for months to get them to stop watching my every move after you ran back to Cincinnati. Anyway, strict Mr. Vanover's long gone, but his much nicer granddaughter took top job a couple of years ago. She thinks there's trouble with kids sneaking into that cave again."

"You probably only think she's nicer because we're a very long time out of high school," Deb said. "I thought the town locked up the entrance not long after our little misadventure."

"Sure did, and that was the first thing I checked once one of my deputies called me in. Still covered with an iron-barred door set in concrete, salvaged from the old jail house. They changed the lock out to make sure no one had a duplicate of the key and everything. Far as I can tell, kids sneak behind the school now without bothering to get into the cave. But school staff keep hearing noises down there."

Deb's eyes drifted toward her bookshelf, where she'd tucked dozens of her Auntie Zelda's colorful and fascinating books in with her own. One of those books had put her on the right track to finding the mountain faerie lair.

"What kind of noises?"

Terri picked up Deb's empty coffee mug and tapped it with her non-existent fingernails.

"Well, that's the part that got my attention, to tell you

the truth. Nothing like talking or scraping. I'm sure you remember how the cave entrance is close to the maintenance shed around back? Apparently one of the janitors was out there for a while setting up a new floor buffer a couple of weeks ago. The whole time, something in the cave was tapping."

"Tapping? Like you're doing right now, even though you know it gets on my nerves?"

Terri stared into Deb's eyes and nodded slowly, continuing her increasingly more annoying random noise.

"Like this, yes. Other folks have heard what sounds like deep breathing, or a rumble like a train was going by under there." She paused—thankfully both talking *and* tapping—as more distant thunder muttered outside. "One of them mentioned it sounded like a thunderstorm underground."

Deb pursed her lips and looked out the window, where the heavy, dark clouds had finally lowered enough to join up with the fog and hide the mountains.

"Has anyone gone down there to make sure something's not going wrong inside the cave? Like an unstable roof, maybe, or flooding from the river?"

"Sure. A couple of my deputies, and a geologist from the college out in Hidden Springs. The way she put it was this cave formed on its own instead of being mined. The rock is pretty much where the rock wants to be for a long, long time, unless humans do something to mess with it. None of them could find a thing to worry about."

"Or to explain the noises," Deb said. "I can't claim to be claustrophobic, since we ran around down there when we were kids, but I'm no geologist or even much of a caver these days. Why me?"

Terri finally set the coffee cup down and pulled the afghan up to her neck.

"Because the other thing they're telling me about the cave

now is how much it creeps them out. One of my deputies is about our age, so he had his own sneaking-around days as a kid. He swears something about it feels *wrong* now. Like something got in there and got spoiled, maybe."

"And you heard spoiled and thought of me?"

Deb smiled when she said it, but her mind was already off and racing. And that old excitement and stubborn curiosity shuffled its feet in the back of her mind, waiting for her to call on it and turn it loose.

"Spoiled stinking rotten if you ask me," Terri said, grinning right back. "But also a damn good investigator who knows how to walk into a strange situation and manage to keep an open mind. What do you think?"

"I think you're getting me into another mess is what I really think. But yeah, I'm interested, as long as the pay rate reflects underground duty and all the clothes I'll probably ruin. You already have a time set up for me to check it out, don't you?'

Terri stood, sweeping the afghan into a neat fold in the same motion.

"You know me too well, cousin. Tomorrow afternoon, two-ish. I hate that I can't be there for this one, but my nephew is getting married up in Lightning Gap. Our family's drama looks like a gentle cough compared to the nightmare of bullshit my in-laws can stir up."

Deb got to her feet as well, already eyeing her aunt's books.

"Why do I get the feeling you missing out on these is going to be a habit? I might call in a bit of backup on this one since you're bailing. I ran into a most interesting woman at the library who lives up the road from here. Turns out she knew Auntie Zelda, and knows her books even better."

"Works for me," Terri said, halfway out the door. "Doubt we can afford to pay her as much as you, between our understaffed department and the broke and equally stingy school board, but we'll work something out."

ESTONOA's high school looked almost exactly the same as it had all those years ago, when Deb was convinced Terri's principal could somehow get her in trouble back in Cincinnati. Maybe using some kind of bright-red Bad Student Alert phone they all carried in their pockets, years before cell phones were anywhere near as common as they were now.

Not that she'd heard of some top-secret Principal's Special Interstate Disciplinary Network app even now, but she wouldn't bet against it.

The two-story brick building sat on a rise, with freshly paved black parking lots all around, and all the athletic stuff out back. A steep, forested hill cozied up the side opposite the road, thick with a dozen shades of green bright from yesterday's rain.

Today the cool air was fresh and clean, with only a hint of the oily odor of recent paving drifting up with the breeze.

The trouble—back when Deb and Terri were kids and apparently again now—was in the steep drop-off beside the row of bright white sheds for sports equipment, groundskeepers, and all the supplies for maintaining the school itself.

No one could see the cave from the road, inside the school, or from the football, baseball, or softball fields. A sturdy chain-link fence ran along behind the sheds too, supposedly to keep the curious from wandering around on the steep, rocky backside of the school grounds.

Except of course high-school-age kids always and forever had their own *underground* network about things they weren't supposed to know about.

Even more so for things they weren't supposed to do, and places they weren't supposed to go.

Deb walked along the line of white buildings, about fifteen feet from the fence but close enough to see the tell-tale signs. A trail of bare, gravely earth hard against that fence, where no weeds or grass took hold even during the riotous growth of early spring.

Evidence that kids were still drawn to that cave and the area around it like moths and millers and all manner of flying critters to the huge field lights during a football game. Even when the entrance was sealed up and locked.

Or at least the grownups thought it was.

That not-at-all-secret path would probably be muddy and slick after the storms yesterday, and nowhere *near* as much fun now that Deb was *supposed* to be back there.

She heard one vehicle pull into the empty parking lot, then another, and turned to see a big green pickup truck and a little white sedan park beside her own sporty blue half-car/half-SUV crossover.

A tidy woman with close-cut curly black hair and dark brown skin got out of the sedan, wearing a peach-colored pantsuit and fabulous matching hat that said just-got-out-of-church loud and clear.

The pickup's driver bounded out with a mass of curly red hair, faded jeans, and a long-sleeved purple t-shirt, declaring Estonoa the home of the Deacons in gold letters. A far better match for Deb's own jeans and denim jacket.

That would be Annie Griffith from the library.

"Principal Vanover?" Deb said, walking that way. "Deb Powers. You probably heard from my cousin, Sheriff Walsh."

The pantsuit-clad woman came to a stop and rolled her eyes so hard her head echoed the motion.

"I *know* you didn't just call me principal, Ms. Powers. Not when it's Sunday, you're not one of my students, and if you'll forgive me for saying so, I suspect you might be a year or two older than me. Why don't you try Gina on for size?"

Annie let out a great guffaw, hard enough that she let go of the curls she was trying to twist into a knot on top of her head.

Deb laughed herself, and knew at once the two of them would end up being friends.

Probably all three of them.

"You have several very good points, Gina," Deb said. "Do you and Annie already know each other?"

Annie grinned and shook Gina's hand, then Deb's.

"Sure, we know each other," Gina said, digging into her pants pocket and pulling out a thick set of keys. "Annie does flower identification hikes for us, and she's led a bunch of workshops the students just love."

Annie finally got her hair wrangled and out of the way, a faint flush blooming on her pale cheeks.

"I mainly talk to them about minerals and rock and herbs and such, and a little bit about different spiritual traditions for world heritage and culture week. They're a great bunch of kids."

Gina flashed a crooked smile and handed the keys to Deb.

"They're great for *you*, thank goodness. But they go above and beyond in their job of giving *me* headaches, exactly like they're supposed to. In fact, I've got piles of work to catch up on for our senior class right now. I know Annie's an experienced caver, and we had everything checked out over the last few weeks as far as safe conditions. We've had more security cameras for back here as a budget request for a while, but we keep getting pushback because the athletic fields and the *front* of these buildings are already covered."

She made her wonderfully expressive eye roll again.

"Okay if you take a couple of radios so you can let me know if you run into trouble?"

Annie nodded immediately, leaving Deb reluctant to admit to the squirmy knot of unease in her belly. She remembered the cave being reasonably level and open for an undeveloped site, with nowhere near enough interesting features to make it worth changing.

But a restless night and weird dreams she couldn't quite remember told her Terri's tales of strange noises had her more spooked than she wanted to admit.

"That sounds fine to me," Deb said anyway. "We'll try not to keep you too long."

Gina shook her head, blowing air out through lips perfectly lined in a slightly darker shade of peach.

"This time of year, you could give me an extra two *weeks* crammed into each weekend and I wouldn't get caught up. I appreciate both of you for taking a look, and for being quiet about it. Speaking of being quiet, I know the people who hear all those noises aren't making things up. They're flat-out not the type. But I have to tell you when the deputies and other folks were down there checking things out, all they heard was the occasional tapping. I'm not sure whether to hope you hear more or not."

She ducked back into her car and brought out two bright orange handheld radios. The stubby gray antennas reminded Deb of tiny little one-piece phones from her own high school days.

"Fully charged," Gina said, and patted a good-sized cream-colored handbag that matched her pearly earrings, necklace, and low-heeled shoes. "And I've got mine in here. We tested them a few days ago throughout all the little chambers down there. You run into any kind of trouble at all, let me know. Sheriff Walsh is out of pocket, but a couple of deputies have an idea what's going on."

Annie and Deb took the radios and turned them on, getting a reassuring blip from inside Gina's purse.

"Sounds good to me," Annie said. "Hope your paperwork goes faster than you think."

"You and me both," Gina said, already walking toward one of the dark red metal doors into the school. "Even though I know better."

Deb tucked the radio into her back pocket, then pulled out the huge keyring. Her slight panic (and hope for a brief delay in going into the cave) faded when she saw how clearly they were labeled.

She held up the one for the gate beside the maintenance shed, with the one marked "Cave" right beside it.

"I need to grab a bag out of my car," she said, "then I guess we're all set."

Annie beamed and nodded, several tendrils of red curls floating free in the breeze.

"Oh good, I'm not the only one who brought stuff with me. Hang on, and we'll set out on our underground adventure!"

Deb grabbed her black backpack, wondering what all an ordained priestess equally comfortable with the pagan side of life—and afterlife—would bring for a caving trip seeking eerie noises.

She'd packed a bunch of the same things the Appalachian creek faeries seemed to enjoy herself.

Molasses cookies, tiny Reese's cups, hard candies with honey centers, and several squares of chocolate and peanut butter fudge Jeff and his father Wayne started cooking the day after they discovered the little critters.

If these were more fairies, or some sort of related creature, she and Annie would have a head start on trying to make friends.

That, a bottle of water, spare hiking headlamps, and her

night-vision goggles rounded out her unexpected caving expedition supplies.

Now if she could only shake her rather unusual case of the jitters, she'd be ready to go.

Annie apparently suffered no such hesitation. She'd already swung a purple backpack that matched her shirt into place and popped one of the little headlamps on under her springy knot of hair. Deb tried not to freak out at the heavy black kneepads in Annie's hand.

Was the cave *that* much lower than she remembered?

Annie laughed and touched Deb's arm.

"Oh my goodness, your face! Don't worry, we can stand up mostly straight in the whole thing. I figured I should bring an extra pair in case we need to kneel down to see something. The rock is murder on your knees."

"Yeah, that's better than what I was imagining." Deb slipped the kneepads into her pack, then pulled the elastic band of her own headlamp over her head. "Do you think we should—"

Deb's words dried up, along with all the moisture in her throat and mouth.

A rapid series of metallic taps rang out from the direction of the cave, made even more creepy by the echoes returning from the rocky slope behind the sports fields.

Followed by what sounded for all the world like thunder and lightning, which made no sense at all under the clear blue sky.

Annie stood with her head tilted, with no sign that her heart was pounding as hard as Deb's.

"I can't pick up any kind of pattern in those taps, can you?" Annie said. "Nothing like Morse code or numbers or anything like that."

"Can't say I hear anything that sensible, no."

Before Deb could think up a way to suggest they try

another day with more people that didn't sound too terribly cowardly, Annie hurried over to the gate in the chain link fence.

"Gina gave you the keys, right? Let's get down there before they stop."

Deb took one look at Annie's bright, excited eyes, and walked over to join her.

No reason she should be this scared, right? It wasn't like some of the cases in Atlanta and around Georgia, when she might be walking into an unexpectedly armed and dangerous situation. Or at the very least an angry one.

Nothing like what police officers faced, but things could get surprisingly out of hand.

Nothing like that here for sure.

Right?

"Okay, let's see if we can figure this thing out." Deb unlocked the heavy padlock, pleased that her hand only shook a little.

The ten-foot climb down to the cave entrance was quicker and easier than she remembered. Someone had carved out steps over the years, and even lined them with rock. While the trail that continued on past beside the fence was indeed muddy and bare from teenager feet, Deb and Annie had no trouble getting down to the flat spot that marked the entrance.

The land continued to fall away below them, but only about another twenty feet or so to a creek that happily splashed and burbled to itself. Deb hadn't heard a trace of it from the parking lot, and now she smelled the mossy rocks, too.

If she had to guess, she'd say a chunk of pale gray lime-stone had crumbled away years ago, leaving a ledge deep enough for several people to stand comfortably. And instead of the chest-high entrance she remembered, half-hidden by weeds and vines that grew fast enough to grab at the ankles of people who stood still for too long, an irregular concrete oval waited.

In the middle, what did indeed look like a salvaged jailhouse door blocked their way. A heavier padlock with an extra-long hasp secured the door to the side bars.

Annie honest-to-goodness bounced on her toes, hands clasped in front of her chest. Between that and her huge smile, Deb might have been down here with a girl who still attended classes in the building up above, with her own opinions about the current-day Principal Vanover.

"I haven't been down here for *years*." Annie reached up and turned her headlamp on, shining it into the cave. "They're doing a great job keeping the steps in good shape."

Deb switched to the right key and opened the lock, shivering at how icy cold the metal was. She turned her own headlamp on, letting the bright white beam play over a narrow passage of gray walls and ceiling. The floor was *sort* of level, if you considered what looked like a jumble of smaller rocks that were mostly smooth on top level.

"Last time I was down here, Terri and I shimmied down the slick weeds late at night, with nothing more than a regular flashlight and a lighter."

She froze, her skin erupting in goosebumps that had nothing to do with the chilly lock and bars.

Now a rising and falling chorus of whispers rushed toward them, with a furious volley of taps close behind. She couldn't catch what direction the noises came from, except that they were all inside the cave.

Annie somehow managed to giggle instead of the scream Deb felt lurking at the back of her throat.

"Wow, they're *excited*, aren't they?" Annie whispered. "Gina was right, things like that happen sometimes when people who are ready to listen show up. We'd better get in there before they get bored with us."

Deb pulled the door open, honestly surprised when it didn't let out a horror movie screech of rusty metal.

"Care to hazard a guess about what *they* might be? I was thinking they might be more of our faerie beasties, but now I don't think so."

Annie grabbed Deb's arm and giggled again.

"You still have to get me out there to see your hillbilly fairies, don't forget. I have no idea what we have here. But I'm not getting any sense that they want to hurt us, are you?"

Deb took a deep breath, taking in the musty, earthy scent of the cave's cold air.

If she really settled down and paid attention—instead of getting caught up in lingering nightmares and all those ghost stories she and Terri and Jeff told years ago—her PI sense of imminent danger wasn't engaged at all.

She felt cautious, sure. Her mind on high alert, all senses tuned up and ready.

But in actual peril, aside from a possible twisted ankle or head-knock on the lower parts of the roof?

"You're right, Annie. I'm not feeling like they want to hurt us either. As long as I don't slip and bust my ass, we should be fine."

Annie laughed again, the sound echoing from ahead of and behind them.

"Still, if you don't mind, I'd like to make sure we're welcome."

"Please, be my guest," Deb said, stepping to the side. Now her curiosity was fully engaged.

Annie closed her eyes for a few seconds, then she raised her head and held both hands up shoulder-high.

"Whoever dwells within this cave, we mean you no harm. We seek only understanding, and to offer help and comfort if it's within our power. We ask only safe passage in return, and any enlightenment you may offer. So may it be."

After several seconds of stillness, the sound of a slow, steady heartbeat drifted out from the cave. To Deb's surprise, the effect was far more comforting than eerie.

Annie clasped her hands together over her heart and smiled at Deb.

"Better?"

"I think it is better now, Annie. Thank you."

They didn't quite have enough room to walk side-by-side, so Deb took the lead. Trying to concentrate on getting her footing on the slippery rocks, holding on to the rough, scratchy walls on both sides. While at the same time looking everywhere in front of them at once and listening for the bizarre noises to start up again once the steady heartbeat faded away.

The rock overhead had tiny stalactites with drops of water sparkling on the ends, but nothing to compare with the big caves Deb had toured as a kid. No bright colors, no spectacular formations.

Only varying shades of gray, and a slow, steady drip of water.

She nearly lost her footing and slipped when what sounded like the world's smallest rock hammer started up in a staccato burst.

In front of her.

Behind her.

On both sides.

Overhead.

She couldn't see a damn thing, but the maddening sound bounced around her skull as much as it did the rocks around her.

Then she heard a long, slow intake of breath, much too deep and long to be Annie or any other person.

And a thousand voices breathed out together from every direction.

Deb turned toward Annie, both of them tilting their headlamps up so they wouldn't blind each other.

"Okay then," Deb said in a low voice. "Did that sound like frustration or relief to you?"

Annie raised her pale eyebrows and shrugged.

"I hate to guess when we just got here, but I have to say I got the slightest hint of impatience. There are a couple of rooms up ahead, then a few more beyond that."

Deb nodded, facing forward again. The main thing she remembered was one of the rooms had a huge puddle in the middle, or it did back then. That was what she'd fallen into and gotten herself and Terri caught.

She'd just stopped beside the first break in the wall to the right when the taps started up again. This time they were deeper, and not nearly as sharp. More like knocks, if the person (or creature) knocking had a big rubber fist.

When she pointed the headlamp into the room and moved one foot that way, the knocks picked up speed, edging closer to booms. She moved the light around, revealing nothing more than a chamber about ten feet square with more boulders than walkable floor.

Not a trace of the remains of teenager parties she remembered from her first trip into this cave. Everything from beer bottles to cigarette butts to food wrappers to far more unsavory discards. Only a few dangling water drops overhead, and a few damp spots beneath.

Deb drew back, and the tension across her neck and shoulders eased along with the noise.

"You getting the feeling whatever we're looking for isn't in that room?" Annie said, a smile in her voice.

"Either that, or it's the *real* treasure room, and something wants to keep it a secret."

The path between the walls opened up, letting them walk together as the noise died down again. The next chamber brought on the same response from their unseen escorts.

It was the third one where things got a whole lot more interesting.

And at least to Deb, a good bit more scary.

This time the tapping and knocking didn't start at all.

Instead a series of long, low sighs built up, one after the other. But this time they had voices to go along with the movement of air.

Voices high and low, of men and women, elderly folks and children.

Rising and falling and tumbling over each other, getting louder with each step Deb and Annie took into the long, narrow room, with walls that sparkled with chips of what Deb thought was quartz.

This ceiling was low enough that Deb had to crouch a little, and she could easily touch both walls with her arms spread wide. The room turned to the left up ahead before ending with a big boulder that might block the way to another few feet they couldn't get to.

Deb turned to Annie and shook her head.

"Nothing up here but more rock. You think it's possible we're providing a good giggle for whatever lives down here?"

Annie scowled, lips pursed and pulled to one side.

"Could be, but something isn't right here. Maybe I'm mixing the rooms up. I thought this one went farther back." She peered around the curve, moving her headlamp all around. "We can check the next one and see..."

At Deb's step backward, the sighs escalated to moans as bone-chilling as any Halloween special effects recording or horror movie soundtrack.

And the rubber fists turned into thuds, huge and heavy enough that Deb's teeth rattled.

She stepped forward again and the sonic assault stopped.

Annie's voice finally sounded as tense as Deb felt.

"Or maybe we're already in the right place."

She moved around Deb, reaching out toward the boulder blocking their way.

Deb glanced down to check her footing and grabbed Annie's arm.

After walking through the whole cave and seeing nothing but dust and damp on the floor, she was looking at black splotches underfoot. Along the dry rocks and in a streak a few inches up the cave wall.

"Something *has* been in here, or someone," she said, then she opened her mouth and drew in a breath. "Do you smell something...chemical, maybe? Like grease or oil?"

She saw Annie's shoulders rise, and her headlamp beam moved as she nodded.

"That's new, and it doesn't make sense here."

The chorus of undulating sighs gradually rose until it was louder and richer than before. Almost like they stood in the middle of a giant group of singers doing warm-up exercises before a performance.

Annie reached out again and touched the boulder.

And the boulder moved.

"What the hell?" she whispered, and pushed again.

This time the whole thing shifted back before one side folded up and swung away.

Deb was surprised her heart didn't stop in her chest when the sighs did.

When she got a look at what lay beyond the fake boulder blocking their way.

Annie stepped past the incredibly realistic painting of a boulder that could have come from the best Hollywood special effects department, and into what Deb only wished were every bit as fake.

Someone had built a series of wooden shelves against the rock walls, out of cheap scrap lumber from the looks of it. They'd even hung what looked like a blue bargain-store tarp above their work area to keep the constant drips at bay.

The stuff stacked on those shelves was anything but cheap.

Several gleaming black handguns tucked in around ordinary hunting rifles with wooden stocks. At least a dozen assault rifles, angular and lethal, and long, curved high-capacity magazines stacked up beside them. Stacks of ammunition boxes of various calibers, and several kinds of silvery tools laid out on a red cloth.

"This has to be some kind of arsenal, right?" Annie said, her hand over her chest. "You don't think someone means to use these *here?*"

The sighs slowly died down to nothing.

"Anything is possible. But my guess is someone's been stealing them, keeping them here until they can find a buyer. From what I know about guns laws in Virginia and states close by, possibly looking for the chance to get them out of town."

"But why here? Right under the high school?"

Deb brought out her smart phone, without a bar of signal but with the thing that mattered most right now.

A camera and a flash.

"Because no one comes down here anymore. Which makes sense. Remember what Gina said about trying to get security cameras for the path down here? As far as the key, I wouldn't be surprised if someone made a copy. Possibly even someone who used to work for the school in some capacity. Either way, I understand why some kind of...*entity* would want someone to know about whatever's going on. What doesn't make sense is *how* we were drawn down here."

Annie shook herself, but her expression remained grim.

"Well, I'm going to see if I can figure that out right now. Go ahead and take your pictures so you can help me."

She swung her purple backpack around and reached inside, bringing out a wad of bubble wrap. Inside was a glass jar full of clear liquid. Another bundle held several tiny shot glasses.

Deb took about a dozen photos before she got out her own treats. Now that she had an idea why they where here, what the true danger was, her curiosity had flared back up full strength.

"Is that *moonshine*, Annie?"

"Of course it is. I figured even if we found something like your faeries or a knocker, from way back in the coal mine days in Wales and Cornwall, they've probably developed our Appalachian Mountain tastes along the way. Scatter whatever you've got around as well and we'll cover all our bases."

They took a few steps back and distributed everything, with Annie filling the little glasses and balancing them on the cave floor. Then she stood up straight and closed her eyes.

"Whoever is here, we offer you our gratitude. We'll take care of the trouble from here, so it will trouble *you* no more. Will you show yourselves and accept our appreciation?"

Deb held her breath, wondering how long this would take, if anything happened at all.

She didn't think the gunrunners or thieves or whoever they were would come charging down here during the day. But she was about ready to get back out into the sun.

They didn't have to wait long.

Whispers drifted toward them from the main part of the cave, like a bunch of students from the school somewhere behind them sharing an especially good bit of gossip.

What gradually appeared in the beams of their headlamps had nothing in common with school kids or the hillbilly fairies.

Shadows rose up from the floor, rippled down from the ceiling, twisted along the walls. Gathered and deepened from pale gray to charcoal to as black as the metal of the likely stolen guns.

Shadows the harsh lights didn't brighten up one little bit.

Deb grabbed Annie's hand and held on tight.

The shadows congregated around the cookies and candy for a few seconds, and the whispers took on the amused sound of laughter. Deb wondered if the faeries around Jeff's house did the same thing when the offered treats fell short of expectations.

Then the shadows swirled toward the shot glasses.

Deb somehow managed not to gasp as the clear liquid disappeared without a drop spilling where she could see it.

She jumped when Annie spoke again.

"I'm glad we brought something to your liking. If we take these things away and make sure they don't return, will you feel comfortable and safe in this place? One for yes, two for no, if it pleases you."

The whispers rose like distant conversation, the words barely out of Deb's understanding, before dropping back to hissing.

One huge knock sounded all around them.

"Then we'll take our leave of you," Annie said. "I hope you will stay, and that I can return to speak to you again."

At another rumbling, single knock, Annie and Deb left the room, and the cave, leaving all their offerings behind.

Halfway back to the entrance, Deb remembered to call Gina on the radio.

"I was about to get worried about you," Gina said, her voice clear as if she stood right beside them. "Find anything?"

Annie and Deb's eyes met, and they ended up giggling for a breathless moment before they could answer. The way the happy sound of their voices echoed and rose and fell all around them with no interference made it abundantly clear the very air in the cave had changed for the better.

"You could say we found something," Deb finally managed. "Do me a favor and call those deputies you have standing by. We've got quite a story for everyone."

LESS THAN A WEEK LATER, Deb had the biggest group in her basement office since the big orange truck unloaded everything and drove away when she first moved in.

Terri took up her usual sprawl on the blue sofa despite wearing her coffee-brown uniform. She'd tossed her somewhat pointy brown hat on Deb's old wooden desk, where it kept strange company with two sleek black flat-screen monitors.

Gina Vanover sat beside Terri in similarly formal attire, even if it wasn't quite as stylish as her after-church peach pantsuit. Deb had to admit her more conventional dark gray version likely projected the authority she needed to deal with a building full of rowdy teenagers in the throes of spring fever.

Annie Griffith, on the other hand, perched like a flowery beam of joy on one of Deb's not-quite-comfortable dining room chairs. Her bright yellow lacy top combined with a gauzy green skirt made her look like one of the teeming masses of daffodils lining the streets of Estonoa with the warm turn in the weather.

Deb took the other angular chair, feeling slightly more dressed up than usual for the office in jeans and a black t-shirt with *Virginia Is for Lovers* across the front, complete with a big red heart standing in for the little v. Her dear sister had sent it along with the coffee mug, a keychain, and a refrigerator magnet.

Probably in a not-so-subtle hint about the state of Deb's love life.

A hint Deb found herself considering taking after the last couple of rather flirty "only friends" dinners with Jeff.

The reason for their impromptu gathering had Deb ignoring her own guideline of not drinking alcohol before dark, one she'd followed for years without knowing why.

All of them held multicolored, normal-sized versions of the shot glasses Annie had used to reward the shadowy beings in the cave. These were vivid blue, purple, red, and orange, and filled with more of Annie's abundant supply of moonshine.

"Before we get into the gritty details," Terri said, "let me just offer a toast to my cousin Deb. Who still insists she will absolutely *not* be getting back into the private investigator business no matter how great she is at it, or how many cases she successfully brings to a close."

Deb rolled her eyes (not as artfully as Gina could), but joined the others in lifting the glasses and taking a healthy sip of moonshine. It went down delightfully smooth but with a spicy hot apple-flavored kick.

Terri shook her head and grinned.

"Annie, if you think you can manage to get me the occasional jar of this, I swear I won't ever ask where it came from. For medicinal purposes only, of course."

Annie giggled and leaned down to pat the half-full canning jar at her feet.

"You're on. I'll even throw in a jar of spring rainwater I gathered last week and charged up with crystals and moonlight. A drop or two of that makes anything taste divine. But only if you'll *finally* tell us what's going *on*."

Terri tipped her missing hat.

"Will do. As it turns out, we got hold of that gun stash before our *interested parties* had a chance to remove all the identifying marks. You probably won't be surprised to hear the serial numbers traced back to theft reports from all over the Commonwealth and neighboring states. Many hours of what I have to say was excellent investigative work led us to four fine gentlemen currently enjoying the generosity of the county's taxpayers over at the jailhouse."

"And one of them," Gina said, frowning, "roamed the halls of my high school a couple of years ago. One I would have optimistically called a great student with loads of potential. I still don't know what went wrong, but he helped himself to copies of those keys. Sorry to say they followed the same damn path the kids still do, walking along the fence from the road. The good news is we'll have those security cameras in place by the end of the week."

"Did you say they *acquired* some of those guns in other states?" Deb said, leaning forward with her elbows on her knees.

Terri held up her shot glass and swallowed the rest of her moonshine.

"I did indeed say that, and you went right to the important part as usual. Didn't I tell you she's a great PI? That little error in judgement put our offenders firmly on the wrong side of a federal statute. So did removing some of the serial numbers. I'm going to do my level best to add on having their little stash on school property on top of all the rest."

"With my *enthusiastic* support," Gina said, before finishing her own shot of firewater. "I daresay that might help me get enough funding to clean our cave up and add it to our geology curriculum. Long overdue if you ask me, or my Poppy. He told me a little story about you, Deb, when I talked to him about all of this the other day."

While everyone else cackled laughter, especially her evil, wicked, and entirely unredeemable cousin, Deb sat back and covered her eyes with one hand. Amazed at the power of an incident from decades ago to heat up her face more than the booze did.

"I can't believe he remembered that. Well, maybe I can, since I still have the feeling all high school principals have supernatural powers of observation."

Gina leaned forward far enough to smack Deb's knee, nodding the whole time.

"I can neither confirm nor deny what you just said, and neither will my grandfather. But I sure do like the way you think."

Annie held up the jar, and not one person turned down a refill.

"I know I intend to spend a lot more time in the high school's fabulous cave getting to know our new friends, with Principal Vanover's permission. We might even be able to use some of our same methods to communicate with your mountain fairies, Deb. Assuming you want to, once I fill you in on a couple of other *unusual* incidents in Estonoa's recent past involving geese and earworms."

Deb laughed at Gina's raised eyebrows, relieved she wasn't the only one who hadn't heard that little story, and maybe not whatever else Annie was talking about.

"Sounds great to me," Deb said. "How about we down our medicine, then walk down to the Railsong Hotel for dinner? My treat, as long as we agree not to discuss my career choices. At least for now."

Deb kept her growing feeling about her career to herself as they all downed their second shots, letting out enthusiastic exclamations about the fantastic apple fire.

Truth was, if the cases stayed as interesting as the first two, she might reconsider leaving her PI days behind.

Estonoa, and her stubborn and persistent cousin and new friends, might change her mind after all.

KARI KILGORE

AUTHOR OF WICKED BONE AND SONGS IN THE MOUNTAIN

DEB POWERS: OTHERWORLDLY PI

THE STRANGE CRITTER AT THE OLD JOHNSTON PLACE

*For Everyone with Unusual Skeletons
in the Family Closet*

THE STRANGE CRITTER AT
THE OLD JOHNSTON PLACE

Deb Powers was a big believer in the power (so to speak) of the right motivation.

She'd put herself through college working too many hours on a computer-training help desk, absolutely determined to keep herself from sinking into debt.

All those hours talking people through their technical difficulties gave her the background she needed for her possible new career as a computer consultant.

Her post-college job as a private investigator rose out of a sincere desire to never have to punch someone else's clock or see her hard work lining a wallet outside her own pocket. Not to mention honing those computer skills to a scarily sharp edge.

She'd turned out to be a much tougher boss than anyone else she'd worked for, but it was worth it.

The mental strain of years of her chosen career as a PI, combined with Atlanta's traffic and heat and humidity created an undeniable need to slow...everything...down.

Between that and her beloved Auntie Zelda's house to

sweeten the deal, the move to Estonoa, Virginia, made all kinds of sense.

And so Deb sat in her cozy walk-in basement office overlooking her lovely new Appalachian Mountain hometown. An office she'd carefully arranged to give her all the flexibility and privacy she'd need to get her new venture off the ground.

Not much need for photos or paintings or other kinds of fussy decorations. Not with big windows showing off the sheltering tree-covered ridge all around Estonoa. Right now the range of springtime green was on full, lush display, creating a wonderful contrast with hilly streets full of red brick buildings.

From the right angle, Deb and any perspective clients could catch a glimpse of the Grasspe River and Oxbow Lake, forming two gentle arcs at the lowest point in town. They also anchored an extensive and beautiful network of hiking trails Deb kept meaning to take advantage of.

Maybe this very afternoon, once she finished meeting with the most interesting prospective client she'd ever had. It was a bit hotter than she'd like out there, but the sun was still high and bright. A perfect day for a long hike along the river, along the cool forest path.

She'd made sure her office wasn't too comfortable, with only a reasonable blue sofa, and considerably less reasonable dining room chairs. All sat opposite the huge old wooden desk she'd kept out of her Auntie Zelda's things. Sturdy and solid, and perfect for giving Deb much-needed distance between her and the people she'd be helping.

That distance and the fully loaded black bookshelves in front of her cinnamon-brown walls would help reinforce her status as an expert, every bit as much as two sleek monitors perched on her desk.

And in the case of this might-be client, she'd thrown every bit of that out the window.

Maybe to land out there with the enticing aroma of her neighbor's sprawling lilac bush.

She glanced at Jeff Denton, sitting only a few inches away, where he'd parked one of her overly angular chairs.

He seemed to be having an easier time staying un-distracted than she was, since he actually focused on one of the monitors rather than stealing peeks at her profile.

At least she thought that was the case. Going by the slow-burn crush he'd developed on her more than thirty years ago —not to mention the one she'd developed in return over the last few weeks—it was a wonder they managed to get any work done at all.

The deep-red hair that caught her attention in her grand-mother's yard all those years ago had faded a bit, but it still grew thick and curly. He'd picked up a bit of silver in his hair and his tidy beard, though he still looked younger than his forty-three years.

He still had every bit of the broad smile and easy laugh that Deb remembered so well. And he certainly filled out his faded Michigan State University t-shirt and slightly newer jeans better than he ever had back then.

Unfortunately she realized too late that he was smiling because she'd missed every word of what he'd just said. Thankfully his bright green eyes twinkled rather than flashing with impatience or anger.

Deb hated to admit it, but she had no idea what he'd just asked her, and no graceful way to fake it past her lapse of attention.

"I'm sorry," she said, smiling herself. "I've got spring fever just like the kids down at the high school. What did you say?"

Jeff laughed and bumped his shoulder against hers. Deb wore one of her absurd number of geeky conference t-shirts, but she'd traded in her normal threadbare work sweatpants for her own pair of jeans. And she might have taken a bit more time than usual trying to tame her wavy brown hair.

"Nothing as good as that," he said. "I was just asking yet another question trying to figure out RAM versus hard drive space compared to processor speed. To tell you the painfully honest truth, despite my geeky tech writer tendencies, I've always just worked with whatever computer the IT department sends me. Same as I did when I suffered in a cubicle under a bank of glaring fluorescent lights."

He looked into her eyes for several incredibly intense seconds, then leaned closer.

"What if I just told you I trust you to pick the best laptop for the job? I know you've got my best interests at heart."

Beth looked away to try and hide her blush, and the growing realization she was moving past crush territory. She had been since the two of them sat together on a decidedly odd late-night stakeout, trying to figure out who was stealing from Jeff's father's house a few weeks back.

A stakeout that led to the far more odd discovery of a tiny little creek-side den stuffed full of the missing items. Inhabited by of what she could only think of as Appalachian fairies

In the weeks since, neither she, Jeff, nor his father had figured out how to communicate with the barely palm-sized creatures. But Deb was enjoying the company—and the increasingly creative attempts—more with each passing day.

Before she could move closer herself, movement in the backyard outside the windows caught her attention. Deb had to bite her cheeks to keep from groaning.

Her cousin Terri, Sheriff Walsh to the county's trouble-makers, with her normal dreadful sense of timing. The very person who'd cheerfully and relentlessly convinced Deb to take on decidedly strange cases over the past few weeks.

Clad in a most unusual outfit for her: a rather flattering sky-blue top with a darker blue swirly, and quite girly, skirt.

Jeff looked that way too, then turned back to Deb with a sympathetic smile.

"Incoming cousin alert." He darted in for a quick kiss on her cheek. "I hope we can get back to talking about our best interests later."

Deb started to get up to let Terri in, and decided to take the unusual step of following an impulse without giving it a second's thought. She leaned close to Jeff's ear, breathing in the warm scent of his skin.

"Sooner rather than later, I hope." And she followed up with a quick kiss of his cheek, right above the perfectly even line of his beard. Before he had a chance to do more than look surprised—and pleased—she walked over to the screen door with what she hoped was an appropriately fierce scowl.

Terri drew back for an instant, then returned the scowl with one of her own.

"Not one word about the getup. I had to go to a bridal shower of all things, can you imagine? Probably because my mother-in-law has never quite forgiven me for not having one myself." She charged right past Deb and took up her normal sprawl on the blue sofa, letting her skirt flare and fall where it would.

"At least I blend in to the only comfortable seat in the place. Got anything to drink? And please, I *beg* of you, nothing that's pink or fizzy or full of sliced strawberries or edible hearts or some other such nonsense."

Terri gave a dramatic shudder, glanced toward the stairs going up to the main floor, and did a double-take so broad and honestly surprised that Deb snorted out laughter.

Jeff only grinned from his spot behind Deb's desk while Terri thumped her sandaled feet to the floor, tucked her skirt around her legs, and turned beet-red.

"How long were you two going to let me carry on like that? Flashing my only gear that wasn't issued by the Commonwealth of Virginia for some guy to see."

Deb grabbed a steel bottle of water she always kept filled in case she (ever) got caught up in her new line of work and forgot to stay hydrated, along with three matching glasses. She filled all three, trying her best to stop laughing.

"I figure until you used your brilliant investigative powers and noticed someone sitting in a very small room."

Terri took the water, but her scowl only deepened.

"I really should pour this all over those shiny new monitors of yours, but I'm about to thirst to death from trying to avoid eight hundred glasses of bubbly sweetheart champagne or true love tingle or whatever they called it." She drained half the glass and sighed, then resumed her glare. "Now I don't feel the least little bit guilty about what I'm about to bring you."

Deb hesitated for a second, not wanting to leave Jeff feeling isolated behind her desk, and not wanting Terri to think it was okay to keep dropping by unannounced like this.

Not that Terri would have cared if Deb told her to cut it out in no uncertain terms.

She settled for sitting in the other dining room chair, right in the middle.

"Since when have you felt guilty about bringing me anything?" she said. "In this case, you even managed to interrupt me at work in my *new* job, helping Jeff figure out how to upgrade his computer setup."

Terri raised one eyebrow and looked from Deb to Jeff, who helpfully held up his water glass in a mock-toast.

"I can get out of your way and stop back by later," he said. "So we can focus."

Deb tried to resist, but she made the mistake of meeting

his gaze. He didn't smile or wink or anything else, but his gaze still somehow turned up the heat in the basement a few degrees.

"Well no, you don't have to go anywhere," Terri said, with a smile that had Deb wanting to warn Jeff to run for it. "This might be something you want to pitch in on, since you both loved all those scary stories we used to tell around the fire. I have to admit this one's got me more than a little bit spooked."

Taking a drink of her own water, Deb wondered what could possibly be more spooky than the shadowy creatures she and her new friend Annie had discovered in a cave under the high school. Eerie as they were, with their noises and their moving shadows attached to nothing but the walls, they'd turned out to be more communicative than the hillbilly faeries so far.

As long as they were given a steady supply of Annie's smooth-as-velvet moonshine.

"I'm not sure I want to get into more of your real-live haints," Deb said. "Not after the last time."

Terri waved Deb's words away, then pointed at Jeff.

"I'm guessing Jeff wants to hear more, just look at him."

Jeff was indeed leaning forward in his chair, eyes sparkling. He shrugged, but Deb wasn't fooled for a second.

"Oh, I don't know," he said. "I'd like to hear more about it I guess, just for curiosity's sake. Assuming it isn't top-secret or for law enforcement ears only."

"But Deb's *not* law enforcement." Terri had a positively wicked gleam in her eye. "She's not even licensed as a PI in Virginia, right?"

Deb resisted the perfectly reasonable urge to reach over and tickle Terri until she cried, or at least until she wiped that satisfied smirk off her face.

Mainly because that very morning, Deb *had* been reading

up on how to get herself licensed in Virginia before her Georgia license expired.

"Okay, I give up," Deb said, shaking her head. "You might end up wishing you hadn't encouraged her, Jeff. Out with it, Sheriff Walsh."

Deb would have sworn Terri *really* wanted to sprawl so she could talk, but she looked at Jeff again and crossed her legs nice and proper instead.

"You both remember the old Johnston place, out toward Timber Haul Road?" Terri waited for Deb and Jeff to nod. "It's still too big and rambling for any normal family to live in, but Cliff Johnston finally figured out a way to use it without violating the terms of the will."

Something tickled at the back of Deb's mind, but she couldn't quite grab it. Jeff asked the obvious question before she could.

"He figured out how to *use* it? What in the world was in that will?"

"Pretty devious and wicked piece of work if you ask me," Terri said. "Cliff's great-grandfather wrote it so the whole family would have to agree before the owner could sell it. Every last one of them. All his kids and grandkids that were alive back then, and that's split up to more heirs as the years have gone by."

"I remember hearing about that now," Deb said, leaning forward with her elbows on her knees, water glass in both hands. "A whole lot of fancy words about the family member who owns it has to live there, and if they ever do try to sell it without all those signatures, the whole thing goes to a trust or something like that? Or I might have just misunderstood a whole lot of fancy rumors, since I didn't even live here then."

"No, you heard about right." Terri shrugged. "And with that bunch, there's a better chance of an extremely chilly day in hell before they'll ever agree to sell it. Not if it helps one of them more than the others, or *any* of the others with a couple of their stingy asses. Anyway, Cliff figured out he could make it into a bed-and-breakfast place as long as he still lives there, and no one can say boo about it. No one who could manage to do anything, at least. Got a very smart lawyer here in town to back him up and everything."

Deb started to pour herself more water, but Jeff somehow stood right beside her with the bottle. She hadn't even heard him move.

"So what's the trouble with it now?" he said. "I wouldn't think a rambling old brick house that's finally *not* empty would be near enough to creep you out, Terri."

Terri frowned as he refilled her glass.

"Not even a little bit. You both remember Cliff? Especially you, Jeff. Couple years behind us in school, quiet, calm and studious. All-around nice guy, and not in the 'no one *ever* suspected *him*' kind of way. About as sane a man as you'll ever find around these parts, present company more or less excluded."

"My level of sanity all depends on who you ask," Jeff said, leaning against Deb's desk right beside her. "Cliff always seemed like a real good guy to me."

"Same with just about anyone you ask," Terri said. "Except for those same stingy and mean relatives of his. He's been questioning his own sanity lately, though, enough that he's started calling in help. Quietly. As in can't leave this room quiet."

Deb nodded and glanced up at Jeff. He held up one hand, like he was about to swear before a judge.

"I won't breathe a word, any more than I have about our little colony of new friends out behind the house."

"You and Deb and your father *have* kept that remarkably close," Terri said with an approving smile. "Annie too. I haven't heard a whisper of tiny woodland tool-stealing creatures out on the gossip vine, and I would have for sure. Cliff's not reporting anything missing, except what he's afraid of in his own mind. But things keep getting moved around from room to room, and in ways that don't make any kind of sense. Before you ask, he hasn't opened the doors to paying guests just yet, and all the renovation is already finished. It's only him up there right now."

"Not like what was happening in Dad's garage?" Jeff said.

That first case had involved tools and socks and food and all kinds of strange things going missing, enough that Jeff finally asked for help himself. And ended up bringing himself back into Deb's life.

Terri gave up and adopted a modest version of her sprawl, kicking off one of her sandals and sitting sideways on the couch, one leg bent. She did take care to tuck her skirt in all around.

"Nothing that makes as much sense, strange as that sounds. Cliff's been finding things like his razor in the freezer. An egg inside his pillowcase, which unfortunately had *not* been hard-cooked first. Piles of salt and pepper in his underwear drawer, potting soil in the silverware drawer, and the remote for the television inside the oven. Apparently he checked inside before he turned it on a couple of days ago, because he melted a pair of his reading glasses in there last week."

"And no one else has been in there?" Deb said. She hated the idea of mental trouble in someone younger than she was, but she knew it happened. She'd seen it in a few sad cases from her PI days back in Atlanta.

"Nope, not until he called me personally to come take a look," Terri said, then pointed at Jeff. "And before you ask, Mr. Security Camera expert, he has them around the outside, but not inside. Those teeny little ones it would be damn hard to spot unless you already knew where to look. He has a point, since folks tend to frown on getting recorded inside a hotel or B&B. He hasn't seen anyone skulking around on any of the recordings."

Jeff held out both hands. "Maybe he'll let us install a few just for this? Help ease his mind? That was pretty much what I expected to do with Dad, until we caught those little critters shorting the cameras out. I still want to know how they *did* that."

"I don't think that would help Cliff feel better," Deb said, another of her more depressing old cases on her mind. "Not unless it shows him sleepwalking, right? I'm going to guess he's afraid he's doing all of it himself but just can't remember."

Terri snapped her fingers and grinned.

"Got it in one, cousin." She winked at Jeff. "See, *this* is why she needs to get back into her old line of work, and I'm absolutely certain the licensing agencies in the Commonwealth of Virginia would agree with me. Cliff's already been to his doctor and to a neurologist. You probably won't be surprised to hear he checks out perfectly normal and sane, at least for someone our age. Or that he doesn't believe a word of them saying he's fine at this point."

Deb only realized she was nodding when Terri flashed her a double thumbs-up, but she honestly had no desire to try to back out.

She could dislike feeling *encouraged* into it all day long, and that didn't make much difference.

She fully expected to head out to the old Johnston place, find nothing strange going on at all, and have to suggest Cliff probably needed medical treatment of some kind. Or more examinations.

Either way, no fun.

And she somehow wasn't willing to turn her back on the case all the same. She was already ticking through which of her Auntie Zelda's wonderful books she wanted to read through to get ready.

"Okay, I'll check it out," she said. "As long as you understand I might not find a thing this time that won't require a doctor to help."

"Any reason I can't come along?" Jeff said. "I actually knew Cliff pretty well back in school. I hate to admit it, but I haven't seen or spoken to him since I got back."

When Deb turned to look at him, he focused on Terri, probably watching for her approval rather than Deb's.

Which was way more annoying that it should have been.

"I don't see why not." Terri got to her feet with her usual careless grace, but still paying extra attention to the unfamiliar skirt. "I figure at this point, you're just paying him a visit. Call it a free stay at what turned out to be a really nice B&B if you want."

Deb stood too, hands on her hips, again scowling at her dear cousin.

"A free stay? You mean this is an overnight job?"

Terri stopped at the door, her eyes twinkling as she looked from Deb to Jeff.

"Didn't I mention that earlier? Cliff says all this stuff happens at night. It's bothering him enough that he's seriously considering selling the place, losing it and all. In other words, sooner would be better. So yeah, if I was officially assigning this job to you, I'd say overnight for sure. Don't worry, he won't charge you a dime."

"He might not charge *me*," Deb said, "but I'm going to charge *you*. And assume you can't make it for this one. Again."

"Not likely, and I honestly wish I could this time. Cliff's place really did turn out great, and I could use some time to myself like you wouldn't believe. I can send you his information once I get to my phone. No pockets in the damn skirt."

"That's exactly why I hardly ever wear them," Deb said. "I think we can manage to find him. What's the name of his B&B?"

Terri stopped with one hand on the screen door, shaking her head.

"He refuses to give it a name with all this going on, or at least he's refusing to tell anyone. Thinks it's bad luck to keep on like nothing weird is happening, you know? Anyway, thank you, Deb. I really do appreciate you."

"But not enough to let me enjoy my new career in peace."

Terri laughed and stepped out onto Deb's miniature porch.

"If I ever see or hear of you working in your new career, I'll consider it."

Deb decided not to argue that she had been before Terri barged in and closed the door instead. Jeff still leaned against the desk, arms crossed, with a strange little smile.

A smile that stirred up a pleasant swirl of warmth in her belly.

"What do you think?" he said. "Mind if I tag along this time?"

"I don't mind one bit, especially since you knew Cliff pretty well. Maybe you can bring a couple of your tiny cameras along so we can cover that base. When can you get away?"

He crossed the few feet between them, standing what would have been uncomfortably close with just about anyone else.

"I'm a work-from-home tech writer, so I set my own schedule just like you do, remember?" He raised one eyebrow in what looked and felt like a challenge. The *good* kind. "I'd be glad to give Cliff a call and check, but as long as I go home and grab a few things and let Dad know, I'm good tonight if you are."

Deb took a breath to give herself time to get some kind of grip on the more...impulsive thoughts careening around inside her head. She hoped the heat rising in her cheeks looked as good as the ruddy flush in his.

"Tonight sounds great to me."

DEB FOLLOWED her usual habit of getting to the scene a few minutes early, parking in a well-maintained rectangular gravel driveway before the sun quite managed to set.

The old Johnston place went against the norm for the area in not showing a single red brick or sliver of white wooden siding. The ornate two-story house rose up in solid gray stone instead, with broad porches top and bottom under the gradual slope of a darker slate roof.

Deb wondered how long it took the stonemasons to make the rounded supports for the railing along the top one. Between that, the lovely angular appearance of the stones, and the curves and arches all over, they'd obviously been artisans equal to anyone working in big cities at the time.

The original timber-baron owners had picked quite a spot, on a big enough rise to set the house apart from the ridge behind it, but keeping most of the yard private. She was sure the brief, stunning view of the house from the meandering main road was no accident, every bit as much as the tall trees along the driveway keeping most of the property hidden.

Someone had cleaned up the overgrown gardens on both sides since Deb's brief visit for a summer party decades ago. Now a series of neat garden boxes formed a grid on the right, with nets waiting along the back row for all kinds of vine-climbing treats. At the moment, only bright patches of early green broke up the dark soil in most of them.

To the left, a winding path led through soft-edged flower beds, with several benches and swings tucked under trees. Only faint floral perfume drifted through on the cooling evening air, but Deb suspected the aromas would be heady and intense by the time the heat of summer arrived.

The fading light cast a reddish tint over the whole scene that would have been romantic under different circumstances. Perhaps still involving Jeff and an otherwise empty B&B for certain.

But with a whole lot less mystery and minus an owner worried about his own sanity, not to mention odd things happening that Deb now knew better than to dismiss out of hand.

A good check through a few of her aunt's books had given her a couple of ideas of where to start, but nothing quite matched up. Not until she had a lot more information.

Her idea that the otherworldly creatures that now called these mountains home had long-since evolved into their own special varieties kept making more sense, even if a few of them had gotten their start across one great ocean or the other.

She heard the crackle and ping of another vehicle on the long graveled driveway, and turned in time to see Jeff's silver sedan come into view. He hadn't hesitated to agree when she suggested they drive separately. Little things like that might be signs that someone had a rough enough breakup to learn a few lessons.

Or—and Deb was gradually allowing herself to believe this after her own rotten split—he might actually be A Nice Guy.

Either way, the unexpected chance to spend this much more time together was a welcome surprise.

He got out with a smile that warmed her all the way down to her toes, and the last bit of sunlight caught the red in his hair and beard.

"Cliff really did fix this place up," he said, crossing over the soft grass to stand beside her. "Last time I was out here, the yard looked a little bit wild."

"I was only out here the one time years ago, and that after dark, but I have to say it doesn't feel any more...off or strange than it did back then. Several miles outside of town and kind of isolated or not, it just seems like a big old house. Unfortunately that probably means the wild things are all *inside*."

Before either of them could say more, the big green front door opened and Cliff Johnston walked out onto the huge porch. He would have looked perfectly at home at any number of Atlanta offices on Casual Friday with his tan golf shirt and dark brown pants. A good match for his corporate-neat haircut and smooth-shaven face.

But something about his grin and the joyful way he bounded across the yard toward them was pure mountains and Estonoa.

"You must be Deb," he said, grabbing her hand in both of his for a quick second. Cliff had a stronger version of the local musical accent, which Deb had noticed could vary greatly within a few miles in the mountains. "I'm sorry to admit I don't remember meeting you all those years ago. Those days were kind of a blur more often than I want to admit. Thank you for coming out here, that means a whole lot to me."

Then he turned to Jeff and gave the kind of laugh that was painfully close to tears.

"I can't believe it's really you, man. I am just *so* damn glad to see you."

Deb was a little surprised to see Jeff blinking too fast with the same kind of laughter.

"It's been about twenty years too long if you ask me," he said, then he and Cliff met in a hug. Pretty typical guy back-pounding-and-kind-of-awkward, but still a hug.

They clearly caught the surprise on her face when they stepped back.

"Jeff, he helped me through some things," Cliff said, shaking his head and smiling. "Sure hope I did the same for him."

"You did, no doubt about it. We need to get caught up as soon as we possibly can. I promise to not be such a stranger, and Dad would love to see you again. Right now I'm hoping Deb can help us both figure out how to help you with whatever's going on out here."

Cliff's smile faded, and he raised his eyebrows and scrubbed his fingers through his short hair.

"I gotta say I hope you can, too. Listen, I know you said you already had dinner, but I set out some good things to snack on while you... Hell, I don't know. Whatever you're going to do. I'll help you with your bags, and you can come on inside and we'll take the grand tour."

He ended up taking Deb's small overnight bag and Jeff insisted on getting her gear bag, with an air of friendly cheer that let her know arguing would be useless.

"Jeff tells me you're a private investigator," Cliff said as they walked through the front door and into the cool air of what felt like a trip back in time. "Or you were back in Atlanta, is that right?"

Deb tried not to roll her eyes too hard, not when she was trying to get a good look at how the grand old house was set up. It was all age-dark hardwood floors and bright, flowery wallpaper, with furniture that managed to look antique but comfortable at the same time. Rich, colorful fabrics, without the hard edges and strange angles that looked better than they felt.

She didn't catch a trace of the mustiness she expected in such an old house. Only the faint, lemony aroma of some kind of cleaner.

"Yeah, I worked as a PI down there for years," she said. "I thought I'd get a change of pace once I moved out here, but Sheriff Walsh is determined to drag me right back into my old bad habits."

Cliff laughed, this time without the tense, bottled-up emotion of before.

"Terri is about as persistent a person as I've ever met in my life," he said. "If she's got her mind made up, you might be better off just going along with her."

They put the bags down at the foot of a grand polished stone staircase that took two right-angle turns on the way to the second floor. A series of warm lights that looked like golden crystals set into the walls and ceiling showed the way.

"I think you might be right," Deb said, then looked at Jeff. "The thing about Terri is sometimes her ideas turn out for the best."

She glanced around the dining room to the right, where a long gleaming oak table that could easily seat ten took up most of the space. An impressive array of knick-knacks and framed photos and tiny ceramic figurines crouched on a heavy sideboard and pretty much every other surface.

A tickle skated along her nerves, leaving her convinced movement followed along just outside of her line of sight in every direction.

Cliff was already halfway down a hallway headed toward what looked like a kitchen, so the only reasonable thing was to follow along.

"I'll keep this room closed up most of the time when I

have guests." Cliff gave an uneasy shrug. "If I ever *have* guests. It's way too modern for the rest of the place."

With all the shiny stainless-steel appliances and counters and white-tiled floor, along with a bunch of high-end appliances Deb didn't even know how to use, he had a point. He'd also set out an impressive array of what he called snacks on a steel table in the middle of the room, alongside a spotless wooden cutting board and a stack of burgundy dishtowels and napkins.

Fruit and nuts and crackers, cookies and bags of chips and a loaf of thick whole wheat bread. He pointed toward the huge double refrigerator behind him.

"Got everything you need for sandwiches in there, and vegetable soup, and cold-brew coffee and milk. I can whip up some mean hot chocolate if you want, and there's ice cream in the freezer. No matter what happens tonight, I really do want you to feel at home."

Deb thought how much Jeff's backyard faeries would have enjoyed the sweet part of this feast. She wondered if Cliff knew about that, if that tale might reassure him.

But the idea fled to the back of her mind when Cliff turned a fearful gaze toward the spotless six-burner gas stove.

"I'd offer to make you something hot, and I'll sure cook you up a great big breakfast in the morning. But I think you're better off not using the stove tonight if that's okay."

Deb perched on a surprisingly comfortable leather-covered black barstool tucked beside the table. Several more waited underneath. Her senses continued their low-level rustling and twitching even though she couldn't see or hear or smell a single thing out of place. Only more of that clean scent, with the warm aftereffects of someone toasting bread and possibly brewing strong tea.

"Terri mentioned you've found a few things in the oven that don't make sense."

After a few seconds, both Jeff and Cliff pulled out their own stools and joined her. Cliff leaned his elbows on the polished surface and rested his chin in his hand. Deb saw weary shadows around his eyes.

"That's a polite way you put it, Deb, not making sense. I can't figure any of this out, and the nightmares starting up are only making it worse. Yeah, the stove has been the worst, but I've found stuff all over the house out of place. Nothing broken or anything like that, except for those eggs inside my pillowcase and the reading glasses I melted into a puddle in the oven. I found a wooden block in there this morning, out of the toybox full of old stuff I put in the library."

He let out a long, slow sigh. "You know that shivery feeling, when you're not getting any sleep and you see things moving out the corner of your eye?"

Deb nodded, wanting him to keep talking.

That was exactly how she'd felt since she set foot inside this house.

"I'm getting that all the time now," Cliff said. "All day and all night. I want you two to be honest with me, okay?"

"You know I will be," Jeff said, and Deb nodded.

"I think you both will be," Cliff said. "Either one of you getting the spooks right now? That feeling like you need to keep peeking over your shoulder?"

Jeff shivered. "I'd just about swear I've got ants walking around all over my skin, and I'm afraid I'll let out an incredibly embarrassing screech if anything touches my back. Never felt anything like that here before."

"Nothing outside at all," Deb said. "But I've been getting more and more jumpy since we came inside too. You're having nightmares now?"

Cliff rubbed his eyes. "That's what's been coming on worse and worse for me. It started out just restless sleeping, which never happened to me all the years I lived in this house. But a couple of months ago, seemed like I couldn't keep my eyes closed more than a half-hour at a time. Then when I finally could sleep, I'd wake up with my heart just *pounding*."

Deb's earlier ideas of wondering about some kind of mental trouble with Cliff faded more with each passing minute, especially since she was getting a near-constant urge to peek over her own shoulder.

"What are the nightmares about?" Jeff said. "Anything you can remember?"

"You mean any of that bad shit I went through as a kid?" Cliff said. "Some of it shows up behind my eyes even all these years later, but that's not what I'm getting now. I can't remember hardly any of them, which isn't like me at all. What I *can* remember is running around all through this house, like I'm trying to find something. Or more like something might be trying to find me."

"Anyone gotten hurt here?" Deb said. "Lately or in the past?"

Cliff frowned. "Nothing beyond the usual accidents and falls and such. Besides all the drama and nonsense over that nasty will and who gets to live here, this place has always been all right. All my bad stuff always happened somewhere else."

"Okay, one more thing and maybe we'll take a look around if that's okay with you," Deb said. "Terri mentioned cameras outside that aren't catching anyone sneaking around, but I have to ask. Can you think of anyone who might want to do something like this? Try to keep you spooked and on edge, maybe move things around? I had one case not long before I left Atlanta where an angry ex got access to security camera footage and edited it to look innocent before the police could review it."

"That's a pretty good scheme," Cliff said with a tired

smile. "No, I can't think of anyone who would bother to do more than fuss and run their mouths. I had a bunch of workers out here helping get things cleaned up over the winter, but no one at all for weeks. Not until I called Terri, and she talked to you."

Jeff leaned forward and plucked a grape so purple it was almost black off of a bunch, then popped it into his mouth.

"Listen, you think you might be able to get some rest now that we're here?" he said. "I hate to say it, but you look almost asleep sitting up. And don't you dare take those bags upstairs either. Otherwise I'll come back and haunt you myself."

Cliff grabbed a couple of grapes for himself and got slowly to his feet.

"I think I might try that very thing in one of the guest rooms now that you mention it. Don't worry, I check my pillowcase and under the blankets now, same way I check the oven before I start it. In case it helps, stuff seems to go missing from all over the house. But it mostly ends up either here or in my bedroom. First door to the right at the top of the stairs. Just in case everything decides to stay quiet because you're here, I made up your rooms at the far end, right across the hall from each other." He walked toward the same hallway they'd come in through, stopping at the doorway.

"I know how all of this sounds," he said, staring at the floor. "Like I'm losing it, no matter what my doctors keep telling me. Just having you two take me seriously is doing me a whole world of good."

When she heard Cliff's footsteps reach the top of the stairs and continue on overhead, Deb stood and turned in a slow circle, letting her gaze play across every shadow and corner.

She couldn't see a single odd or creepy thing when she looked directly at all of it.

But she got a stronger and still-building sense of all the activity happening barely out of her line of sight.

"Right there with you," Jeff said, now standing and turning in his own circle. "I didn't want to make Cliff any more upset than he already is. But I'm paranoid and jumpy as hell in here."

Deb let out her breath and bumped her shoulder with his.

"I'm glad it's not just me. You knew him way better than I did. What do you think? Anything like what happened to him before?"

Jeff faced her, but his gaze kept moving around the room, a lot like her own wanted to.

"He seems tired and kind of beat up, but okay. Nothing like when he had trouble back in school." He finally managed to focus on her. "Pretty much a typical story, I guess. He got into a bad situation with work of all things. A bunch at a sawmill that's not there anymore. I think all they wanted was to pressure Cliff into letting them come up here and clear it all out. It's hard to see in the dark, but the land is covered with trees that haven't been touched for a long time."

He rubbed the back of his neck and glanced around again.

"The worst part was his family got angry with him over the whole thing, with those assholes from his work making it worse. It all took a pretty bad toll on him. He ended up staying with me and Dad for a few weeks to get away, and that mill went belly up not long after. They'd hatched the whole scheme to try to stay afloat. None of that helps explain what's going on now."

Deb gave in and turned her head from one side to the other again. On a normal night, she'd say the bright lights overhead and along the counters and work surfaces didn't cast more than the normal number of shadows in here.

Right now, she'd say those shadows trembled in place, just waiting for her to look away so they could get busy.

About as far from the deliberate, sort of *thick* shadows she and Annie had discovered in the cave under the high school as they could get.

"You and your father did a good thing for Cliff," she said, taking his chilly hand in her warm one. "Let's see if we can do another one. I don't like this idea much, but I'd like to kill all the lights in here and set up with my night vision goggles."

"And hide in the corner and see what we can see. I don't like it either, but it does make sense. Want a cup of that cold brew Cliff mentioned?"

"You bet," Deb said, squeezing his hand. "Might want to give it a sniff and make sure there's not shampoo or something mixed in."

By the time she got back with two sets of goggles and a low-light camera from the bags (that were indeed still all the foot of the stairs), Jeff had two heavy white mugs on the table beside all the food.

And he sat on the stool again, staring wide-eyed toward a couple of feet of space between the big refrigerator and the wall.

"I might not admit this to someone who hadn't seen the critters behind Dad's house," he said in a low voice, "but I'd just about *swear* something is hiding back there. A whole lot bigger than our Appalachian fairies, too."

The uneasy chill that skittered along Deb's spine was matched by a jolt of excitement. She might not ever admit it to Terri, but she'd already adapted herself and her driving curiosity to investigating bizarre creatures more than enough to enjoy the chase.

She stepped closer and whispered close to Jeff's ear.

"Maybe whatever we've got is waiting for the room to

clear out. How about you take your goggles and put them on, then stay put. If this critter is comfortable enough that you *saw* it moving, you getting up might set us back." She handed him the set of what looked like black, rubbery bug eyes. "I'll turn lights off in here and in the rest of the downstairs, and get back here as quietly as I can."

Jeff nodded and leaned toward her, the motion small but unmistakable.

Deb brushed her lips across his ear, kissed his cheek, and ended with the corner of his lips, with the stiff hairs of his beard tickling her.

He grinned up at her, then pulled her down for a quick but electrifying kiss full on the mouth.

"Now I've got goosebumps for all the right reasons," he whispered. He slipped the goggles over his head and nodded. "Sitting duck, ready for action."

"And a very cute duck you are."

Deb slipped her own goggles on and stopped at the door, flipping three light switches down at once, leaving nothing but the ghostly glow of a microwave clock and assorted tiny appliance bulbs.

Jeff sat unmoving, head aimed at the empty space.

The lights were only on in three of the rooms besides the entry and the kitchen, so Deb only needed a couple of minutes to plunge a sitting room, a room full of crowded bookshelves that had to be the library, and a low-key living room with a well-disguised television into darkness. She flipped her own larger set of goggles on and walked through the faintly green glow back to the kitchen.

She realized she'd been every bit as careful and quiet as she imagined when Jeff jumped at her gentle hand on his back.

Instead of speaking, he shook his head and pointed toward the gap he'd been watching before.

Deb looked that way, and immediately got caught up in a rush of bizarre sensations as her body flashed hot and time slowed to a crawl all around her.

Something walked around the edge of the refrigerator, on two legs and wearing a tiny dress, with a decidedly old-fashioned kerchief around its pointy-snouted head.

The whole creature stood about as high as Deb's knee.

She couldn't be sure with the goggles—not to mention the way her heart pounded in her chest hard enough to make her vision shake—but she thought it had dark body hair and a lighter face.

The hands looked almost...human at first. Four stubby fingers and a thumb, but with a needle-like claw at the end of each one. Sort of like it was wearing dark gloves and letting the pale fingers poke through.

Clutching what looked like an ordinary, bright-yellow tube of lip balm of all things.

But when it walked on toward the stove, Deb saw its feet were bare. And not the extended toes of a chicken, like some of the mythological creatures she'd studied earlier in her Auntie Zelda's book.

These had four toes facing front, and what looked sort of like a blunt, clawless thumb off to the side rather than a big toe.

Almost like the foot had a thumb set too far off. A thumb made for gripping things.

She looked back at the face, which was nowhere near as pointy as she'd assumed. This was rounder, with a black nose at the tip, and whiskers to go with soft, rounded ears.

It was the long, naked tail trailing along under the skirt that finally made the whole thing click together in her mind.

Deb leaned so close that her lips touched Jeff's ear, but she suspected he found that anything but a turn-on in that moment.

"I'm going to block that gap with a cutting board. You want to grab a dish towel and try to push it into the oven?"

Jeff shook his head slowly back and forth, but he turned to whisper against her ear, which was indeed *not* a turn-on.

"I'll do it anyway, but with oven mitts. Be ready for a very possum-like scream, and not from me."

Deb smiled despite the surreal situation, glad he'd seen the same thing she had.

A tiny little possum-woman, walking without a care through the modern, neat kitchen.

Preparing to stash a stolen lip balm in the oven.

Each of them moved at the same time, with painful slowness as far as she was concerned.

Meanwhile Possum Lady casually tucked the lip balm under her arm and reached up, standing on those amazing back toes until she could reach the oven door handle. She hauled it down, stepping back at the same time, then hopped up onto the door.

She walked forward, her fleshy feet making quiet little squeaks on the oven's window glass.

Deb picked up the big cutting board and kept going, while Jeff grabbed a handful of dishtowels after all.

The oven mitts were now on the bottom of that open door and out of reach.

Everything worked perfectly, and quietly, until Deb went to put the cutting board beside the refrigerator.

It slipped out of her sweaty hand and clattered against the steel side.

She turned in time to see Possum Lady jerk up and whirl, with a truly intimidating number of sharp teeth bared.

Jeff darted forward with a shout and shoved the oven door closed, skidding full length onto his back on the white tiles underfoot.

But he managed to keep one hand on the oven door and hold it steady.

Where an unearthly hell of a scream rang out.

"Close your eyes!" Deb ran to the light switches as fast as she dared without ending up on the floor herself. She closed her own eyes, flipped the lights back on, and pulled her goggles off.

Jeff moved to sit with his back against the door, pulling his own goggles off.

Then he covered his ears against the horrific shrieks.

"I don't think she's very happy with us," he said, raising his voice. "Can't say that I blame her."

Deb burst into laughter at that, putting her goggles on the big table before she dropped them.

"You'll make a fine PI yourself someday, Jeff Denton, with powers of observation like that. What the hell do we do now?"

A series of thuds sounded above their heads, which Deb seriously hoped was Cliff heading downstairs rather than a herd of reinforcements of the critter variety.

"She's about to push this door open behind me, which I won't hear once she screams me deaf. Block the other passages, close the door, and hope she'll talk to us like your typical civilized possum wearing a dress if we let her out?"

Deb snorted and turned just in time to see Cliff charge into the room and do a pretty good skid himself before he caught the edge of the table. His black-sock feet matched the scruffy t-shirt and baggy shorts, and he'd somehow managed to muss his corporate haircut to go with the pillow creases across one cheek.

"*Please* tell me that's not one of you! Unless that screaming is coming from *inside* my oven?"

"We're fine," Jeff nearly yelled. "But I think you might

have to replace this fine appliance by the time we're all finished here."

"Want to shut the door?" Deb said. "Then help me block off any escape routes?"

Cliff stared for a second, mouth hanging open, before he closed the door. While Jeff shifted to his knees and kept a firm hold on the oven door, Deb and Cliff used another cutting board and several big sheet pans in an attempt to secure the area.

"Ready?" Jeff said when they stood on either side of him, Cliff wearing the black oven mitts and Deb holding a gigantic steel pot that she had no clue what to do with.

When they both nodded, Jeff got slowly to his feet, leaning against the oven the whole time. He moved to the side and opened the door a tiny crack.

The screaming stopped at once.

Ears still ringing from the sonic assault, Deb mouthed, "Now what?"

A high, raspy, whispery voice floated out of the oven, with the thickest mountain accent she'd ever heard.

"Reckon maybe you could let me out of here, and we'll see what we can't get worked out?"

"I... Well yeah, I can do that." Jeff grinned like an extremely handsome fool. "You're not going to scratch me or bite or anything like that if I do, are you?"

"I sure do see why you might think that of me," Possum Lady said. "But seeing as how I'm the only one squished up inside a box with hardly any room to move, *I* ought to be the one asking *you* for promises."

"Fair enough," Cliff said, now smiling himself with the same dazed sort of wonder Deb felt. "But please do talk to us, ma'am. I hope we can come to some kind of agreement between us."

Jeff stepped as far to the side as he could before he pushed the oven door down.

The lip balm came flying out and *pinged* off the metal table.

Followed by the Possum Lady herself, with ears laid flat like a pissed-off cat as she smoothed her soot-streaked skirt and adjusted her kerchief.

She stood with hands on rounded hips and glared at Deb and Jeff.

"Never have seen the two of you before," she rasped, then focused on Cliff, who still held his oven-mitted hands at the ready. "You're the one making all these dang *changes*, ain't you?"

Cliff nodded like he was sleepwalking.

"I am, yes. Cliff Johnston, and I sure didn't mean to upset you. If you don't mind me asking, ma'am, what are... I mean *who* are you?"

Possum Lady tapped one of her fleshy foot-thumbs, then crossed her arms.

The movement pulled her dress against her body, showing what Deb was certain was a u-shaped row of tiny breasts.

"You just call me Warcha now that you're all big and grown. I'm the one meant to guard over you, have been since you were a tiny red-faced screaming baby. Thought I'd be right back to it once you come back home, least until you had young'uns of your own."

Warcha stamped her foot on the glass, making a little smack.

"But *no*, you had to go and make a mess of things." Her voice rose closer to her piercing screech. "Fixing it so I get lost trying to walk from one room to the other. Can't see no reason nor rhyme to it at all. And you bring in a great old big bunch of *strangers* I never did see nor hear of before."

Warcha shook her head, with her rounded black ears lifted a little bit closer to normal, and her voice quieted back to its whispery high pitch.

"Now I know I ought not to get mad like I did, and start moving all your stuff from here to there. But so help me, I couldn't *see* straight with all that foolishness going on."

Deb put her cooking pot on the table and held up her hands.

"I'm so sorry, Warcha, but with everything going on, I've lost track of my manners. I'm Deb Powers, and this is Jeff Denton. We're only here to help Cliff and see if we can figure out a way to keep both of you happy. Are there more like you here?"

Warcha sighed and let her hands drop to her sides.

"Not right now there's not, with only one of you to check on. Is that what you got planned with all this disarranging?"

Cliff blinked and stepped forward, lowering his hands, mitts and all.

"Well, not babies and such, no. At least not right now. But I was going to have all kinds of company coming in to visit for a few days at a time. That's what I've been doing, getting ready for that. Will that help bring...new ones?"

"I can't make promises for what I don't rightly know." Warcha looked from one to the other of them. "Reckon I can do my best. There's bunches of my kind don't have any people to guard now. Might be happy to help out."

Deb fought to keep her giggles contained for a change, not wanting to upset Warcha when they'd just met. But the idea of a bunch of little Possum People running around underfoot made it a hard struggle.

"Will the guests be able to see you, Warcha?" she said. "And the other ones who might show up to help?"

Warcha gave a tiny possum head shake, and Deb had a sneaking suspicion she rolled her jet-black eyes.

"You ever seen me, Cliff? Before tonight and all this foolishness? From whisker to tail?"

"I can't say that I have, no," he said, slipping the oven mitts off and scratching his spiky hair.

"Well there you go." Warcha looked at him for a few seconds, then lowered her head. "I'm right sorry I treated you in such a way. I won't no more now that we got to talk. You about finished with all the moving and switching around?"

"I guess I am now that I know it bothered you," Cliff said with a laugh. "Maybe you can let me know what you need without all the stealing? And the nightmares?"

Despite the much calmer mood and the lack of things moving around at the edge of her vision, Deb stepped back when Warcha climbed down off the oven door.

She stood, hands again on her hips, staring up at Cliff. Her slender tail brushed back and forth on the white tiles, again like an annoyed cat.

"Don't reckon I need all that much, but I sure will let you know if you'll do the same. Now that I can get back to guarding and taking care like I'm meant to do, things'll go a good bit smoother around here." She stared at all three of them before she turned toward the refrigerator. "Think you might unblock my path there so I can get back to my work? This time of year, can't turn my back on the ants and mice and spiders for a second, less they overrun the whole dang house."

Deb blinked, then took a couple of shaky steps over to the refrigerator. When she lifted the cutting board out of the way, Warcha strolled across the floor like she didn't have a care in the world.

She raised one little hand without looking back before she disappeared.

No one moved for what felt like a hundred years, even

though Deb still heard the almost-normal beat of her own heart.

"I don't have any earthly idea what to say after all of that," Cliff finally said, his grin returning. "Except do y'all want some real food, and maybe some hot chocolate with a shot of something stronger in it?"

All three of them fell to laughing even harder than before, clutching their bellies and wiping at their eyes before it was all said and done.

"That sounds fantastic," Jeff said. "As long as you let me help."

"Me too," Deb added. "And maybe answer a question or two."

Cliff walked over and peered into the gap beside the refrigerator, then opened the door and pulled out a glass bottle of milk.

"I'll do my best, Deb, but you know as much about this whole situation as I do. Some of that vegetable soup and grilled cheese sandwiches okay? I have to admit I'll feel a whole lot better about using the oven once I've had a chance to give it a good scrubbing."

Jeff put his arm around Deb as they laughed together.

"That sounds just about perfect to me, Cliff," he said. "And probably about the only thing that might let me get to sleep tonight, but I doubt it."

Deb slipped her arm around his waist, wondering if she would manage to close her eyes if she ever got into bed at all.

She had the feeling none of them would sleep one wink tonight, but for good reasons for a change.

"Soup and sandwiches it is. Then I'll bring in my Auntie Zelda's book and see if we can't figure out what you've got here. I have a feeling *we'll* be writing the books on this one someday."

KARI KILGORE

AUTHOR OF WICKED BONE AND SONGS IN THE MOUNTAIN

DEB POWERS: OTHERWORLDLY PI

AN EDDY OF THE UNEXPLAINED

For everyone who wonders what waits
Just beneath the surface

AN EDDY OF THE UNEXPLAINED

Deb Powers suspected no one in her new hometown of Estonoa, Virginia, would be more surprised to see her actually *working* at her new consulting job than she was.

She sat in her endlessly distracting basement office, with views of the beautiful town rolling down and away from her. The big windows were equipped with both blinds and curtains, to keep her double monitors and other computer equipment from being *too* visible.

And honestly to keep Deb from worrying about what she wore on particularly casual (or lazy) days, or when she puttered around down here late at night.

But she couldn't bear to block that view during the day, not when she could look across town and watch the constantly changing light and shadow and rain and fog playing along the curving ridge that sheltered Estonoa.

Right now, much earlier than she was usually at work, a drifting mist fluttered through the deepening green of late springtime, dancing in and out of the trees like it was playing hide and seek. Deb knew the fog would burn off long before noon when the heat of the day set in.

That only made the teasing effect that much more enticing. And distracting.

For the first time in ages, though, Deb paid full attention to the big monitors on her old-fashioned wooden desk. Her Auntie Zelda had used the desk for Deb's whole life, for an infinite variety of purposes.

Studying for her degrees in history and antiquities when she wasn't much younger than Deb at forty-two. Plotting out her research trips around the world, to explore folklore and belief systems in different cultures. Writing her several books on the subject, all of them tilted toward her fellow travelers and those who were simply curious, much more than toward her fellow academics.

All of those volumes and hundreds more waited on the overstuffed black bookshelves that lined nearly every wall in the basement. Deb just about had her aunt's books memorized, with their breezy prose and vivid, detailed descriptions. But she knew she'd return to them again and again, along with the massive collection of other books on the same subject and more.

Partly because she'd long been fascinated with how humans interacted. How they worked and lived, loved and fought. That interest had served her well during her years as a private investigator back in Atlanta.

She never would have believed she'd be turning more and more to the folklore and strange creatures references once she moved to Virginia and attempted to take up a new line of work.

The line of work she was finally actually doing with her new friend Annie Griffith right that very minute.

Annie perched in one of the embarrassingly uncomfortable dining room chairs Deb kept in her office, mainly to prevent potential clients from staying too long. She'd stopped just short of begging Annie to take her own comfortable high-tech chair instead.

With her typical joyful and enthusiastic nature, Annie had refused. Claiming she was only there to ask enough questions to get on Deb's last remaining nerves. While Deb was there to think and plan and generally be brilliant while she designed Annie's first proper website.

"So you can set it up so people can make appointments with me on the website?" Annie said, brushing her impressive tumble of red curls back over her shoulder. "And the site will let me know when they do, *and* put it on my calendar?"

Deb switched to one of the demo sites she'd set up weeks ago in a burst of enthusiastic preparation, before she'd unexpectedly gotten pulled back into her old line of work. With Annie along for one of the most interesting and surprising cases.

"You bet," Deb said. "See how it has certain hours and days blocked out, and the others are available? You set that up yourself, to make sure no one can double-book or try to get you to work on your day off. Then when they do schedule, it notifies you right away."

Annie shook her head, her pale cheeks coloring a bit even though she was smiling. Today she had on one of her trademark gauzy, flowing tops in purple, paired with sturdy black hiking pants and boots. Since the plan was to finally get Deb down onto the network of trails around the Grasspe River that brought visitors to Estonoa year-round, Deb dressed the same way. But with a geeky movie t-shirt instead.

"I've seen those calendars on websites for hotels and such," Annie said. "But I had no idea it was something I could afford and learn how to run for myself. I thought it needed big servers and all kinds of programming, and more money than I could afford to throw at it."

Deb smiled as she booked an appointment on the calendar, then switched to her email on her second screen. As soon as the message popped up, Annie let out an irresistible giggle.

"No worries at all on any of that," Deb said. "It's gotten a lot easier over the years for sure, and I'll make sure you understand how it all works. As much as you *want* to understand, anyway. And the cost will be quite reasonable for my hiking and cave-full-of-mysterious-shadow-creatures buddy."

Neither Deb nor Annie were quite sure what the creatures they'd found under the high school were, even though they'd been visiting them regularly since their discovery. What they *did* know was that adventure had led them to a stash of illegal weapons that were now off the street, along with the criminals who had hidden them there.

"Well, I can tell you I've got plenty of friends who prefer to focus a lot more on their work than their websites," Annie said. "And they'd be thrilled to have someone like you who they can trust to help them with it. I was thinking I'd like to sell a line of..."

Annie broke off, head held to the side and a distant look in her eyes. Deb had seen her do that a few times, and it always meant something weird was about to happen.

She had no idea if that was Annie's training as an ordained priestess, her deep knowledge of pagan and all kinds of other faiths, or something she'd simply been born with. But in the few weeks they'd known each other, Deb had learned to trust it.

Or sometimes to dread it.

"You've got company," Annie said with a mischievous grin. "Or you will in a minute."

With no surprise whatsoever, Deb looked out the window just as a brown-uniformed figure turned up the sidewalk leading to her office door. She didn't have to look twice to recognize Terri Walsh.

Sheriff Walsh to most people in Estonoa and the surrounding area.

And Deb's often-annoying and much-loved cousin Terri.

"Ten to one she's got something she thinks I should investigate," Deb said, with much less irritation than she used to feel at the idea. "And yet another reason I should finish getting my Virginia PI license."

Annie laughed and shook her head.

"No way I'm taking that bet. From what you've told me, the better odds are that she'll *really* wish she could go with you, but still have an inescapable reason why she can't."

Deb's laugh was much closer to a guffaw, one she barely managed to get under control by the time Terri knocked on her screen door.

"Whatever it is," Deb called, "I didn't do it."

Terri let herself in, taking off her stiff-edged hat that managed to be rounded and pointy at the same time.

"I've known you way too long to believe any bullshit about you being innocent." Terri tossed her hat on one end of Deb's wonderfully puffy and inviting sofa, then flopped down herself, arms and legs going in all directions. "Good to see you, Annie. Great to see you, as a matter of fact."

Annie turned her head just enough to flash a hidden wink at Deb.

"How's it going, Terri?" she said. "Got something interesting going on?"

Terri ruffled her fingers through her wavy brown hair, but it somehow fell neatly back into place. Deb had given up on ever learning that trick for her own disobedient hair.

"*Interesting* is such an ill-defined term, don't you think? I mean in the sense that we're supposed to want *interesting* things in our lives all the time. The older I get, the more I crave a little bit of predictable day-to-day routine. Not happening on this day, though. You make it down to the trail here in town yet, Deb?"

Annie stood and carried her chair back in front of the big desk before Deb could say a word. The only thing she could think to do was walk around herself and turn the other chair to face the couch as well.

"Not since I moved here," Deb said. "There wasn't much to see when you dragged me out there for a party when we were kids. Annie was going to take me down there as soon as we finished up. I'm going to set her up with a new website."

"Is that right?" Terri's eyebrows went up, and she smacked her own leg and grinned. "You mean you're actually doing your long-rumored consulting job, and I'm lucky enough to witness it?"

"Yeah yeah, smartass. I set Jeff up with a new computer a couple of weeks back, remember? You should, you barged in and interrupted that day too."

That day Terri had interrupted more than a consulting job. She'd thrown a wrench into what Deb hoped was the next phase of the slow-burn flirtation between herself and Jeff Denton, a long-ago friend of both of them. Terri also sent Deb and Jeff on a case that day, ending with the most unusual surprise member of a household any of them could have imagined.

"I do seem to recall something about a setup between you two," Terri said, pursing her lips in a (fake) regretful pose. "One that's still in progress if I'm not mistaken."

Annie snorted at that, leaving Deb not sure which of them to be more annoyed with.

"Just say it, Theresa."

"You got it, Deborah. Even though you haven't yet made the effort to enjoy our trails since you moved here, I'm assuming you know at least a little bit about them."

Deb sat back and crossed her legs.

"I *do* have family here, which shouldn't be a surprise to you since you're one of them. I know they opened the trail in the first place because there's a good bit of history there. You're not going to tell me someone's been seeing ghosts of the Baron and his sweetheart?"

Terri waved her hand in Deb's general direction.

"If that was happening, you know the town would have been all over it on all the tourism sites. Probably those ghost hunter shows would have already descended to stir up all kinds of trouble. This is out on the other end of the trail, toward Marlene's Eddy."

Annie shivered and raised her shoulders for a second.

"That's an incredible spot, very powerful." At Deb's puzzled look, she went on. "It looks like the river tried to divert into a different path, but it only cut through the softer rock. A little ridge of bedrock kept it from going any further. But it did manage to carve out a wonderful little rounded channel, almost like a whirlpool."

"That's the place." Terri picked up her hat and brushed at a bit of something Deb couldn't see. "I don't know about powerful, but it's very pretty there. Quiet too. Anyway, these last couple of weeks, hikers have been reporting unusual things around the eddy."

Deb could tell herself all day long she didn't want to return to her high-stress life as a private investigator. That she'd made the big move to the small town to help herself along the path to making a career change at the same time.

None of that stopped her constantly curious and active mind from latching on to every strange thing Terri gave her, like an obsessive hound dog with a good squeaky toy.

"Strange how?" she said, refusing to throw out suggestions for Terri to shoot down. Partly because she enjoyed the surprise too much.

"This one really is hard to put into words, even for me,"

Terri said, frowning and looking serious for a change. "People say they feel...threatened lately. Even people who've been hiking that trail since it opened four years ago. They swear their skin crawls, like they're being watched. Not just people, either. Their dogs get freaked out and don't even want to walk through there. It's strong enough that several people have called us in."

"Did you take police dogs out there?" Annie said. "To see how they react?"

"We did, or we tried to. These aren't fresh-out-of-training dogs or officers, but the dogs refused to get within twenty feet of the eddy. They didn't bark or alert, they simply stopped walking." She paused, staring up at the ceiling for a few seconds.

"I was out there myself this time, and I had people checking the water, the brush, the trees, all around the area. I saw with my own eyes that it's safe from anything I know how to investigate. And I'm not afraid to admit my skin was about to crawl right off until I walked far enough that I couldn't see the eddy anymore. This sounds crazy, but I know you and only about three or four other people in the world would understand. Something is *wrong* there, to the point that I'd support closing that part of the trail until we get it figured out, tourists dollars lost and angry county voters after me or not."

Deb felt like her own skin was going to crawl off from the tense, agitated expression on Terri's face, and the tight sound of her voice. Whether it was her love of telling scary stories around the campfire when they were kids, her wild days as a teenager, years as a patrol deputy, or her duties as sheriff, she'd never known Terri to be afraid of much of anything.

Besides stirring up the wrath of her in-laws, anyway.

But Terri was at the very least deeply spooked.

"Okay, tell me the truth," Deb said. "If we decide to look into this, do we need someone with us for protection? One of your deputies, or *you?*"

Terri swung her legs around and sat up straight, staring down at the floor. Deb only then noticed that her normally spotless black uniform boots were coated with dust and mud, likely from the trail around Marlene's Eddy.

"My gut tells me this isn't a matter of *physical* harm," Terri said, still looking at the floor. "What's got me shook up is feeling like someone who's not prepared could run into some other kind of trouble if that makes any sense. I didn't even hear any animals or birds, and I was out there for a few hours." She looked up at Annie. "Could someone intentionally...I don't know, harm an area? Break it somehow, make it cause this kind of discomfort?"

Annie blinked and sat back, tilting her head to one side. Then her brow drew down and Deb was certain the temperature in the room dropped by several degrees.

"The idea of someone intentionally making an area cause harm, or even creating the impression that it *could* cause harm, would be a truly serious matter. Rising to the level of a crime in many circles. Think about it. If someone did that on purpose in a public space, they'd have no idea who would end up getting hurt. That feeling of threat you're talking about could be enough for someone to trip and fall at the very least."

Terri nodded slowly, rubbing her chin.

"That's why they're calling us. That feeling of threat. People are afraid bad things have already happened, or that they just haven't happened *yet*. So you're saying that's unlikely? Or that you hope it's not true?"

Annie held both hands up in a warding motion, and Deb was sure she felt an odd ripple of movement, like that wasn't simply an empty gesture.

"I'll always hope something like that isn't true. In this case, I suspect it's unlikely as well. But if folks are feeling it so strongly, especially if you are, someone needs to figure out what's going on."

She turned to Deb, looking more curious than challenging.

"What do you think? You're the trained investigator Terri trusts on these kinds of bizarre cases. I'll do what I can to keep us safe if you think you're the one for the job."

Deb didn't bother trying to hide her smile, but she managed to keep it fairly small. For the first time since she'd shut down her PI operations in Atlanta and headed north, she wanted nothing more than to jump right back in.

"You *bet* I want to check it out. When can you be ready?"

All traces of Annie's thunderous demeanor vanished when she grinned.

"Give me thirty minutes to go back to the house and get what I need, and I'll pick you up on the way back through town?"

"Works for me," Deb said. She turned to Terri, with a good idea what the answer would be before she asked. "You joining us, cousin?"

Terri turned her hat in her hands.

"I know you think I'm full of shit half the time when I tell you I can't make it, or you might think I just don't want to. This time I've been out on the trail all morning, and I've got an inhuman amount of work stacking up. What I *want* is for this to be investigated and fixed if it possibly can be. The best way to get that done that I know of is to turn you two loose. I'll clear it with park personnel to close that section of the trail to anyone else."

"I'll take it." Deb stood, already planning which of her Auntie Zelda's books she would pull out to study up while she waited for Annie. "We'll let you know the second we have something."

~

THE DRIVE DOWN to the trail and most of the hike out toward Marlene's Eddy passed in a sort of horrified haze for Deb. She wasn't sure whether Annie's tale of Estonoa getting attacked by earworms or sinner moths was worse, or whether she wanted to hear *any* more stories of the town's history.

She'd never imagined reality actually surpassing the crazy tales she, Terri, and Jeff scared each other with on so many long-past summer nights.

She also had her first real misgivings about settling down here, but they didn't last long.

After all, strange and freaky and just plain weird as Atlanta could be, Deb wasn't likely to find anything nearly as interesting as she'd already discovered in her newly adopted Appalachian hometown.

The section of the trail heading to Marlene's Eddy ran parallel to the Clinch River, running heavy and hard after a bunch of springtime rains back when she and Annie first ventured into the cave under the high school.

The light brown water danced and splashed over rocks Deb couldn't see, and climbed a good way up thick sycamore trunks lining the banks. The air was cooler than nearly a thousand feet higher by her house, but it felt at least a thousand times more humid.

Thankfully it was too early in the spring for mosquitos to be out. A bright, cheery buzz of less-maddening insects accompanied them, along with the mineral scent of fast-moving water carrying a load of mud and silt.

The trail itself was packed gravel, and someone obviously kept the weeds trimmed before they could get much of a foothold along the sides. Terri and Jeff and Annie and everyone else had been telling the truth about how much Estonoa cared about their river and the trails all around it.

Deb promised herself she'd ask Annie the names for the bunches of wildflowers growing in the sunny spots, and all over the steep hillside further up. If she asked right now, while she was more uneasy than she wanted to admit, she'd forget everything before they got back to her house.

One thing Deb knew she *wouldn't* forget was how fresh and wonderful the water Annie brought for both of them tasted. Water caught during the same storms that had the river running high, then "charged up" in the sun and moonlight, as Annie put it. Whether it was magic or the absence of the heavy load of chlorine in the tap water, Deb couldn't remember simple water charging *her* up like a sip of this did.

Annie stopped, one hand on Deb's shoulder. She'd wrangled her crimson curls into a near-halo on top of her head, and the sunlight sneaking through the thick canopy of trees only increased the effect.

"Do you hear that?"

Deb opened her mouth to ask what she meant, then she caught the different sound of the water up ahead. Not exactly quiet, as if they'd come to one of the smooth, tranquil stretches of the Clinch River. This was noisy still, but more *organized* somehow. Moving, but without the energetic chop.

"Is that the eddy?"

Annie nodded, adjusting the straps of her purple backpack. She'd shed the gauzy blouse in favor of a surprisingly plain black t-shirt. A pendant that looked like the pale face of the moon—with closed eyes, a nose, and a mouth—hung on a silver chain around her neck, with an oval orange stone and a round purple one underneath.

Deb couldn't possibly explain why, but something about

that pendant made her feel far more safe and secure in a strange situation.

"Just around the bend in the trail," Annie said, pointing toward a narrow passage tucked in beside three massive sycamores that had grown together into one vast trunk. "I don't exactly know what to expect from the way Terri was talking. But I'd say it's possible one or both of us will feel more than a little uneasy. You ready?"

Right at that moment, Deb was busy wishing she'd packed a few of her Auntie Zelda's books rather than trying to keep her own black backpack light. She'd furiously skimmed through several of them before Annie got back, but none of the water spirits or sprites or anything else like that matched what Terri described.

She tried not to dwell on how much she hoped they were *not* walking toward some version of Annie's sinner moths with no ghostly guides around to help.

"I'm probably not ready, no," Deb said. "But let's go anyway. The town won't put up with part of a trail this beautiful being closed, sheriff's orders or not."

Annie smiled, but without her normal openness.

The fact that she seemed worried rather than excited only gave Deb's nerves fuel to burn even higher.

"Between that and the town not wanting word of some kind of trouble getting out," Annie said, "I suspect we're on a tight deadline no matter what."

They walked on together, and Deb made sure to touch the smooth bark of the huge sycamore as she passed by, same way Annie did.

She only had a few seconds to marvel at the incredible setting of Marlene's Eddy.

The trail arced to the right away from the river, closer to the tree-lined hillside that it had anywhere else.

To the left, a broad oval of water did indeed move almost like a whirlpool.

The little ridge of moss-covered gray stone that made the whole thing happen stood firm and unyielding against time and the surging river. A gap upstream dipped down several inches and a couple of feet across. Enough to let a driving stream of water escape the main channel, at least for a little while.

The water swirled against the harder rock's contours, splashing up enough to escape in spots, but not much. Enough to feed more thick, deep-green moss, and let a miniature forest of several different kinds of ferns prosper around the edges.

The bottom of the circling pool was invisible in shadows, or maybe it was covered with silt or more moss. A mystery the river might drop low enough to expose sometimes, or maybe one always kept hidden away.

A lip of rock at the downstream end of the eddy was covered in what looked like strands of dark green hair that fluttered as the water escaped to rejoin the river it had so hastily abandoned.

The edge of Marlene's Eddy was wide enough for a few sturdy wooden benches, and Deb thought how enchanting it would be to sit there and watch the water enter, explore, and defeat temporary capture.

But that thought only lasted long enough for her senses to catch up with her surroundings.

Possibly bringing more than her typical five into service.

A chill far deeper than the tree shadow could explain worked its way through her bones and muscles, surfacing as raised gooseflesh and hair standing on end.

An irregular circle of flattened weeds and flowers showed where Terri and her deputies had walked through the area, but that didn't lessen the intense feeling of something just out of sight.

Not even a little bit.

Something it would be a mistake to ignore or even attempt to get comfortable with.

At the same time, a weird disorientation darted through Deb's mind. Trying with all its might to convince her that her feet were slipping under her, or maybe the land itself was shifting to get in on the fun instead.

"Are you...I don't know, feeling dizzy?" Deb said, settling her feet into a wider stance. "This is almost like trying to keep my balance on a rocking boat."

Annie frowned, looking all around where they stood. Deb noticed she stood firm and steady as well.

"The energy here is a *mess*. You know how you put earbuds in your pocket, and they come out a tangled disaster no matter how careful you are? This seems like that to me. The bad thing is this part of the trail normally feels rock solid. Like you could stand on one foot for an hour or do a handstand, and never feel the least bit tired."

Deb's body threatened to pitch to the side despite her efforts to stay put.

"I can hardly stand up straight right now. What could cause energy itself to get knotted up like this?"

Annie knelt and swung her backpack to the ground— moving as if she was trying to stay upright on solid ice.

"That's a damn good question. With places like this, it's usually the circling water that keeps it feeling so grounded. So solid. Pulling your body and your mind and everything else into closer contact with the earth. I can't *see* anything here that should have upset that balance."

She pulled out several quartz crystals a few inches long, ranging from totally clear to pink, red, cloudy green, and dusty golden, and lined them up on one of the triplet sycamore tree's roots running along the ground. The mottled brown surface was thicker than Deb's waist.

Annie carefully arranged the crystals so they were parallel to the river, rotating and moving each one until only one facet seemed to barely touch the wood. Deb was sure they'd topple over if she so much as blew toward them.

Then Annie pulled out what looked like two doubled pendants on short silver chains.

Despite her disorientation, Deb grunted in surprise.

"Those are pendulums, aren't they? My Auntie Zelda had one that looked just like that."

"Your Auntie Zelda had this very one." Annie grinned and held one out to Deb.

One end was shaped like an incredibly detailed tiny acorn, about half the diameter of a dime. The other end was an equally lifelike oak leaf smaller than Deb's thumbnail.

"Zelda got me started on my path," Annie went on. Her pendulum had a miniscule apple chained to a rounded apple leaf. "I've been blessed to study all over the world, and with bunches of amazing teachers. But so many things I learned from her I've never heard a trace of anywhere else. In this case, I brought her that pendulum back from Wales. Did she show you how to use one?"

Deb nodded, blinking back tears that took her by surprise.

Her auntie had been gone for several years now. She'd had a resurgence of grief when she first moved into the house, but she thought it had shifted into happy memories again.

Holding an object she knew her aunt loved and always carried with her brought up a heady mix of loneliness and joy.

"She showed me how with this, and with her crystal ones." Deb held the silver leaf between her thumb and forefinger and let the acorn swing free. "When I tried it years ago, it turned in a circle for me when the answer was yes. Then it switched to back and forth for no."

After several seconds of breathing in and out slowly, trying to clear and quiet her mind, the acorn refused to do anything but jitter in every direction. The fact that Deb's hand stayed rock steady made no difference at all. She twined the chain through her fingers.

"I don't think it's working," she said, turning to Annie.

Who was getting the same response from her little silver apple.

"I've brought both of these out here several times," Annie said, standing with her pendulum between her thumb and middle finger, eyes closed. "Normally I get the same as you, circle for yes, back and forth for no. Marlene's Eddy is usually so powerful on its own that all mine do is spin in the same direction as the water no matter what. The effect is powerful enough that I've brought new ones out here to clear them for myself and for people I work with."

Deb was alarmed to see Annie tilting gradually to one side, but she caught herself before Deb would have reached out to steady her. Annie opened her eyes and turned her palm up to catch the apple, then closed her fingers over it.

"Something is *agitated* here. Disturbed enough that people who normally don't pay any attention to such things are feeling it. I was hoping these would help us. Did Zelda ever show you how to use one to find things?"

Deb smiled. "She sure did. That was one of the things I used a lot when I was a kid, but I got out of the habit later on." She let her acorn swing free again, but it immediately resumed its chaotic motion. "I would think about what I wanted to find, then ask if it was in the room where I was. Once I got the circle for yes, I asked which direction. I can't say it worked every time, but more often than not, I went right to what I wanted."

"She taught me the same," Annie said. She slipped her pendulum into her front pocket, then knelt again, trailing her fingers in the water circling through Marlene's Eddy. "It's not going to work for us here."

Deb tried closing her eyes and focusing on keeping her hand still while the pendulum moved, but a wave of nausea crashed through her, all the way from her gut up to her jaw. She blinked her eyes open and shook her head, putting the tiny acorn and leaf into her own pocket.

"I'd swear I have a bad sinus infection, or maybe an ear infection. No wonder the dogs are getting so upset. What do you think caused..."

Deb trailed off at Annie's gasp, and she followed Annie's wide-eyed gaze.

All the crystals Annie had so carefully balanced on the sycamore tree's root no longer faced the same direction, parallel to the river. Now they pointed every which way, and a dark gray one had fallen onto a patch of puffy moss on the ground.

"I used to bring crystals out here to clear them too," Annie said, folding her arms so she held both elbows. "Not one of them has ever moved once I balanced them there. I'm sorry, Deb. I have no idea what's going on."

Deb opened her mouth to ask what felt like yet another useless question, but her breath caught instead.

Annie still stared at the jumbled crystals, and she made no move to straighten them or pick them up.

But she was again tilting to one side.

In the same direction she had before.

And Deb had the strangest certainty that if she closed her own eyes, she'd lean the same way.

Her gaze went back to the crystals, and her heart sped up

when she realized the gray one in the moss pointed the same way.

"Hold still, Annie. Nothing's wrong. I just want to take a look at something."

Deb took enough steps to put herself on the opposite side of the eddy from Annie, with her boots almost in the churning brown river.

She looked toward the wooded hillside and picked out what she thought would turn out to be the right direction, focusing on a spot where one slender poplar tree had fallen against a much bigger oak. The dying tree still had the distinctive rounded, four-lobed leaves on its branches, but they were drooping.

Likely a victim of the big spring storm Annie collected their water from.

"Okay, do me a favor," Deb said, closing her eyes. "Watch me for a few seconds and see what happens."

The river's churn jumped right into her stomach, and Deb gritted her teeth to keep her lunch where it was supposed to be.

"You're tilting," Annie said, "like you're trying not to fall into the river. If you're not careful, you will anyway."

"Now look at the hill back there, and see if you can draw a line between the eddy and me. I'm curious where it ends up."

Deb heard Annie walk away and push though the growth beyond the trail, and willed this part to go faster. A rotten sense of not-quite-spinning joined the nausea, as if something inside her head moved in the same kind of chaotic, random motion as the pendulums.

"Okay, I'm standing in the spot. Better open your eyes, Deb. You're taking on an unhealthy shade of green."

Deb opened her eyes, but focused on the river for a few seconds. She tried to imagine letting her internal disorientation float away with all the branches and leaves and runoff.

When she turned, Annie stood perfectly framed between the sturdy, living oak tree and the ruler-straight beam of the dying poplar propped up against it.

"See anything strange out there?" Deb called, heading that way.

Annie turned in a circle, her gaze aimed at the tops of the trees around her. She repeated the same thing looking at her head height, then again at the ground.

"I'm not sure what I'm looking for. Unless you mean this poor tulip poplar." Annie took a few steps toward the bottom of the downed tree. "Looks like the roots just let go and it rolled right over."

Just as Deb reached her side, Annie abruptly dropped to her knees, whipping out her cell phone.

"*Please* tell me you see that," she said, aiming the phone's narrow white flashlight beam toward the tangle of small roots and mud that supported the tree until they couldn't any more. "That jagged bit of...something white and broken under there. A lot paler than the roots."

"I see a lot of roots," Deb said, leaning forward with her hands on her knees. "I think most of them pulled loose from the ground instead of getting broken. But what you're aiming at, that doesn't belong. There's something else there."

Deb stepped close enough to the brand-new muddy hole full of the woody connections where the tree had drawn its lifeblood that her feet slipped and squished under her.

But she spotted a section of pale yellow that looked too straight and too sharp to be part of any kind of root. Especially not the pliable roots for a tree that still hadn't realized it was dead yet.

Annie scooted forward until she could shift her legs

around and slid down into the hole, with her feet on either side of the jagged thing.

"Deb, I think this is a bone," she breathed, twisting herself to fit deeper into the space. "I can't say for sure, but it looks too thick and heavy to be much of anything else but a human thighbone. Snapped right in half."

"It was *under* the tree? How the hell did it get down there?"

Annie started to reach out to touch the jagged bit, then drew herself back.

"I don't think whoever owned that femur got themselves down there at all," she said. "My guess is they were put under the ground a long time ago, and the poplars came later on. Maybe even the oaks. I've never seen anything like this within a few hundred miles of here outside of an old family cemetery or two that people forgot to keep track of."

Deb managed to get her own phone out and pointed toward what she was now certain was a femur. She'd be willing to bet a brighter bit she caught in the light—poking through the rich, reddish soil a couple of inches away—was the other end of the bone.

Now that her eyes knew what to look for, she spotted other things that didn't belong. Edges natural, but too rigid and sharp.

The distinctive curve of a skull, a parallel line of ribs. A scatter of small pieces that could very well be a clenched hand that had long left the flesh of life behind.

"I know I'm getting way out there now," she said, "even after everything I've seen over the past few weeks. But is it possible this *caused* whatever's wrong out here? I don't mean it made the tree fall. Maybe these bones turning up made a difference, though. Makes the whole thing real for someone, or something."

Annie took several quick photos of the bones and

climbed out of the hole with a hand-up from Deb. She stood muddy and shaken, staring into the long-forgotten grave.

"I think it's a lot more than possible, Deb. If we'd had even one more good rain over the past week, or if an animal jumped in here to hide, these bones would have disappeared again. Probably forever. It seems clear to me someone on this side of the veil or the other very much wanted to make sure that didn't happen."

They stood beside the long-lost grave for several long, solemn minutes.

The Clinch River still muttered to itself, and the endless circling of Marlene's Eddy continued, along with the faint rustle of leaves in the canopy overhead. Now the rich smell of newly turned earth rose up stronger than the scent of muddy water, both with an equal promise of new life and things long passed into another state.

The absence of sound from birds or wildlife Terri mentioned earlier now felt more fitting than forboding.

Deb wasn't particularly worried about where her own mortal remains ended up. But the idea of someone who *did* care, and who might have been so desperately unhappy and alone for decades or longer left her shivering.

"Should we say something? Or do something? Once I let Terri know what's going on, this whole area is going to become at least a low-key investigation scene. It still feels out of balance for sure, but at least right now it's peaceful."

Annie nodded and walked back to get her backpack. When she rejoined Deb, she held the gray crystal in her free hand.

"You noticed which way this was pointing, right?"

"Yeah, but not until I noticed *you* were tilting the same way. My stomach was jumping around about as much as your pendulums for a minute there."

"That's *your* pendulum," Annie said with a smile.

"Even if Zelda hadn't asked me to make sure you got it when the time was right, I would have made sure you had it. Hold this in one hand, since it helped point the way for us."

She gave the smoky gray crystal to Deb, then knelt to rummage through her purple backpack. Deb gratefully took the chance to brush a few tears away.

Her Auntie Zelda's chain and charms in her pocket couldn't have been worth more to her if they were made of pure gold.

When Annie stood, she held a small green carved-glass jar with water inside in one hand, likely more of her storm-caught rainwater. Her other held a bunch of leaves and petals of all shapes, sizes, and colors. Some dried, others that looked fresh.

She poured about half the leaves into Deb's free hand, then closed her eyes and breathed deeply for several seconds.

"We may not ever know who you are," she said, "or how you came to linger in this place. Yet we stand in this place ready to wish you peace and an easy passage to wherever you may be heading."

She nodded, and Deb scattered her leaves and petals among the bones while Annie did the same. Annie poured water from the sparkling blue jar across the whole pit.

"May you know the strength, wisdom, and endurance of the oak," she said. "And may the straight trunk of the poplar guide you along the bridge between this world and the next, while serving as a balm to your soul as you're properly laid to rest. So may it be."

"So may it be," Deb echoed.

In the time it took for a sigh, a flutter of wings sounded from over their heads. Deb couldn't see anything, but the unmistakable voice of a cardinal sang out a series of bright and exceedingly normal "What *cheer!*" calls.

Then she spotted a squirrel darting up a maple tree not too far away.

Annie pulled her own pendulum out and held it up.

It still showed the same random, jerky movement as before.

But the tiny apple showed an unmistakable arc of a circle at the same time.

The clear sign for *yes*.

"Well, this spot may not be quite back to normal," Annie said. "That might not happen at all, or not until this person's bones are handled with respect and care. I have a dear friend over in Bountyfield who might be able to help us with that, the same one who helped me with the sinner moths. Still, I'd say you and I made a difference already."

As they walked back to the trail and headed for home, Deb heard a second cardinal answering the first. Leaves rustled off to the left before a pair of striped chipmunks dashed across the trail in front of them.

Then came the melodious flute-like song of a wood thrush, the doubled notes rising along with the hair on Deb's arms.

She knew anyone else passing this way would feel the change as clearly as the animals did.

And they'd all understand it was a change for the better.

"I think we made a difference too. Let's get Sheriff Terri on the case and see what else we can't get done to lay our mystery bones to rest."

KARI KILGORE
AUTHOR OF IN THE PINES AND SONGS IN THE MOUNTAIN
DEB POWERS: OTHERWORLDLY PI
FINDING THE TRACKS TO THE PAST

For all my fellow train and ghost enthusiasts

FINDING THE TRACKS TO THE PAST

Deb Powers was beginning to suspect she'd made her distractibility problem worse rather than better.

She currently sat in her back yard outside her basement office, under the shelter of her greatly expanded porch. What had been a postage stamp-sized concrete pad and tiny roof barely big enough to hold one chair and an umbrella now stretched a good fifteen feet to the right of her office door.

The new porch floor also stretched several feet further out into the yard, leaving plenty of room for an outdoor sectional couch, two chairs, and a porch swing, all fitted with cheery blue and green cushions.

She hated to admit it, but those cushions were deep and plush enough to be more comfortable than her sofa inside the office.

Right now, late in the Virginia mountain spring and early in the afternoon, the porch was open to the warm breeze. But rolled up and nearly hidden under the edge of the roof hung screens that would connect with magnets, letting in air and light while it kept pesky mosquitos and other flying creatures out.

Deb even had a set of clear plastic covers to hang up when the weather turned cold in the fall. And there was still plenty of room in the big back yard of her Auntie Zelda's house for a modest gas grill and plenty of flowerbeds.

Creating an outdoor paradise, especially in a town as pretty as Estonoa.

From where Deb sat on the porch swing—beside her more-like-a-boyfriend-every-day friend Jeff Denton—she could look out over the sheltering ridge that surrounded the town. Her house perched on the highest edge, giving her a view of all the red brick buildings spreading out below, with bunches of brilliant green trees and colorful banners accenting the scene.

She even caught a glimpse of the sparkling water of the Clinch River twisting along the edge of Estonoa, anchoring miles of trails and a state park that drew people here for recreation all year long. Also the location of a most unusual discovery involving an eddy that seriously disturbed people and animals alike.

The banners informed all those tourists and locals that the annual Chow Down on the Clinch festival started tomorrow. As if anyone within sniffing distance needed any reminders that something special and mouth-watering was coming up.

Someone had a meat smoker going full strength, and the enticing aroma of baking bread floated along the breeze as well. Deb was pretty sure she'd caught a whiff of cooking onions earlier, which she was determined to sample no matter what sort of dish they were destined for.

Before she could say anything or ask about the festival, Jeff's father Wayne lifted his nose in the air like a good hound dog sitting in one of the chairs. Both Denton men wore blue jeans and t-shirts to go with sturdy work boots. Deb wore much the same thing, with her wavy brown hair wrangled under a faded blue handkerchief.

Once work on the porch finished a couple of hours ago, they'd all abandoned their toolbelts in favor of celebratory glasses of beer brewed right there in Estonoa.

Wayne had the same curly hair as Jeff, but his had lost every trace of Jeff's red to snowy white. He still had the same twinkle in his eyes, though, and the easy good humor. Wayne also had the musical local accent stronger than his son did.

"I don't know how on earth you can get any of your computer work done, Deb, not with all that good cooking smell floating right up into your yard. Pretty as your porch turned out, you might have to head back inside to get your wits about you."

Deb managed not to laugh too hard at that, mainly because she'd been having a heck of a time focusing on her supposedly new career as a computer consultant since she moved to Estonoa a couple of months back.

It all made so much sense in her mind, especially when she was near-desperate to get out of the rush and hustle and busyness of Atlanta, and the ongoing stress of her years as a private investigator.

Move to her family hometown, into her dear Auntie Zelda's house. Change gears and careers, and downshift into a much calmer and more reasonable lifestyle. Use her brain in a different way for a change, with computers and websites rather than tracking and chasing and investigating.

But she'd never quite managed to get beyond setting up her fabulous basement office, with a wall full of big windows that lent itself to distraction almost as well as the porch.

"I hate to admit I get pretty distracted with the view inside my office, Wayne," she said. "And the computer business keeps taking a back seat to my old line of work."

Investigating a steady stream of disappearing tools at

Wayne's house was the first thing that pulled Deb back into PI work. That overnight stakeout had revealed a far stranger cause for the trouble than Deb or anyone else could have imagined.

And created the first time she'd seen Jeff since they were both teenagers, which became more of a good thing every day.

Wayne grinned. "That reminds me. Unless I'm forgetting about something, those tiny little critters in my back yard have returned everything they pilfered out of the garage and the house. I keep leaving out the candy and cookies and such, and they keep taking everything sweet. But I haven't had a single new thing go missing."

Jeff nodded and pushed the swing into gentle motion. Deb probably wouldn't have believed her own eyes if he hadn't been with her that night. When they discovered a den full of glowing green mountain faeries or pixies or something like them, surrounded by all the things they'd been stealing from Wayne.

She hoped they'd figure out a way to communicate with them eventually.

"They haven't shorted out any more security cameras either," Jeff said. "I'm not sure if they're happy with Dad now, or just bored with both of us."

Deb took Jeff's hand and gave it a squeeze, wondering if he got the same increasingly pleasant tingle every time they touched lately.

The kisses they indulged in more and more often turned the tingles into fireworks.

"We might have to liven things up for them," she said. "See if that gets them to communicate more."

Movement caught her eye before she could think up anything fun to suggest.

An all-too-familiar woman wearing faded blue sweatpants and an Estonoa Deacons t-shirt that might have been new when Deb and Jeff were in high school. Deb in Cincinnati, Jeff here in Estonoa, and a good bit over twenty years ago.

Deb's cousin Terri Walsh, sheriff and bringer of all manner of curious happenings that kept pulling Deb right back into her PI ways.

Terri stopped in her tracks, scowling and tilting her head to the side.

Deb tried, she really did, but an overly loud snort of laughter escaped anyway. Jeff and Wayne joined in with a little bit more restraint.

When Terri left for a week's vacation, the porch was its former miniature version. Deb realized with a bit of a shock that she really had made the decision to expand her outdoor space, accepted the Denton men's offer of help, and gotten it all finished in one exciting (and exhausting) week.

Shaking her head, and still scowling, Terri kept walking. Rather than turning onto the short sidewalk that led to the basement office's door, she plowed ahead to the new relaxation spot.

"So tell me," Terri said, standing in the middle of the porch, hands on her hips and looking around, "did you purposely decide to make all these changes while I was gone so you could sit there and watch me wonder if I'd turned up the wrong street?"

"Well, I didn't do it all in a week just to confuse you," Deb said. "But I have to admit that's an unforeseen bonus for all the hard work. You just get back into town?"

Terri leaned over and poked at one of the green cushions on the couch, then the blue one beside it. She shrugged and flopped down into her normal dramatic and somehow graceful sprawl.

"Nice couch. We got back late, late last night. I slept like the dead, but it takes me at least two weeks to fully recover from a week spent with my in-laws. I swear those people could turn a marble statue into dust in an hour with the sheer force of all the hot air and nonsense gushing out of their mouths."

Jeff laughed under his breath and shook his head.

"I'll ask the obvious and indelicate question then. Why do you go on vacation with them? Doesn't sound to me like you got to relax."

Terri blew air out through her lips like a horse.

"Of *course* I didn't relax. I'm about as far from relaxed as I think a human being could possibly be and still be more or less coherent. The problem is they've got me all figured out, and that includes my insufferable jerk of a husband. They pick places they know I won't be able to resist and things they know I'm dying to do. This time it was New Orleans, and the French Quarter, and swamp tours, and Cajun cooking classes. Which you will all appreciate when Deb throws a porch-warming party and turns me loose in her kitchen."

"Oh, I don't know," Wayne said, winking at Deb and Jeff. "Sounds like a great vacation to me. What have they got planned for next year?"

Terri rolled her eyes. "Next year? I should be so lucky. They were plotting and scheming about a trip in *October*, which they refused to tell me a single thing about. They know I'll have time to work up my resistance if they give me too much warning."

Terri tried to hide it, but Deb caught the sparkle in her cousin's blue eyes.

She didn't doubt Terri's in-laws were exasperating, as so many in-laws managed to be. She also knew Terri wasn't the sort to do a single damn thing she didn't want to do, and how absurdly smitten she and her husband had been since the day they first laid eyes on each other.

"I hate to ask," Deb said, "but if you're so wiped out, what are you doing here? Not that I'm not glad to see you, of course."

"If you were glad to see me, I expect you would have offered me one of those refreshing beverages all three of you are enjoying." She stared at Deb, gradually widening her eyes until Deb pointed at a bright red cooler at the foot of the couch.

Terri got up with an exaggerated sigh, fetched herself a bottle, and let Wayne open it.

"I suppose that will have to do," she said, resuming her sprawl and taking a sip. "Anyway, I went in to work early this morning to try to catch up before Monday. No one else was supposed to be there, so I figured I'd actually get some work done without drowning in the post-vacation flood of bullshit."

"That explains the remarkably casual clothing," Deb said. "Even I wouldn't be caught out and about in a getup from...what, the Reagan years?"

"Second Clinton term, thank you very much. Which is last century, yes, but not all the way back to the Eighties. So I did manage to get through a small mountain range of paperwork before someone came wandering in. Have you heard from Gina Vanover over the last couple of weeks?"

Gina was the high school principal in Estonoa, and thankfully much less strict and forbidding than her grandfather had been in the same job. Though Deb supposed if Gina had been the one to catch her sneaking around the high school over summer break—and when she didn't even *attend* that high school—the response would have been equally stern.

Probably more so.

She and Gina had become fast friends since Deb and her other new friend Annie helped with a distressing situation at the high school.

"I haven't seen her for a couple of weeks," Deb said. "She's not having trouble with those shadow creatures in the cave again, is she?"

"No, nothing like that." Terri set her beer on the concrete pad, kicked off her ugly pink rubber clogs, and stretched her legs out. "This is...it feels a lot more personal. To Gina and to me. You know the old train depot in town? Down near the river?"

Deb nodded, pushing the swing back herself this time.

"Yeah, I've seen it. Beautiful old building, in rough shape last time I really paid attention, which was when you dared me to run up and touch the door if I remember right. One of those 'if these walls could talk' kind of places from what I hear about the partying that used to happen in Estonoa."

Wayne laughed, and Deb saw Jeff smile at his dad out of the corner of her eye. Jeff also took the chance to reach for her hand. Tired as her own hands were from all the work building the porch, the warmth of his fingers felt wonderful.

"Partying is an awful gentle way to put it," Wayne said. "I can just barely remember the depot being open, back when trains still stopped here. My mom and dad had stories about all the coal miners, timber workers, and railroad folks rolling into town to spend all their money quick as they got it."

"Spend it all or die trying in quite a few cases," Jeff said. "But I also heard it was quite the hot rendezvous spot, especially for couples who decided to run away together."

"Sounds like you all know plenty." Terri grinned, no doubt relieved her own time as sheriff didn't include constant brawls and debauchery all along the railroad side of town. "Thing is, Gina got a bunch of people together a few months ago to start renovating that old depot. Bunch of grant money, too. Several towns all through the mountains have done that, turned them into community centers or museums or even classrooms. Everything had been going great until the last week or so."

Deb tried not to shiver, thinking of the strange, peculiarly Appalachian creature she and Jeff had discovered in a newly renovated B&B not that long ago.

"Did Gina tell you what's happening?" Deb said.

Terri took another big swallow of her beer and scooted around on the couch until she sat cross-legged and facing forward.

"Not until this afternoon. But she's been calling in reports of trespassing that don't make sense all week long. Things knocked off shelves or knocked over. Footprints all through the dust, inside and out. Tools moved around, doors either locked or unlocked, day and night. Same with windows. Got a few complaints of noise from people who live nearby, too, when no one was there working. Dead in the middle of the night."

"Charming choice of words," Deb said. "Your deputies checked it out?"

"Of course they did. Couldn't find a trace of anyone sneaking around, not outside of what Gina reported. I hate this for her, but apparently nothing happens when one of the patrol cars hangs around. That kind of thing can drive you crazy."

That was the other part of the incident at the new B&B. The owner, Cliff Johnston, had been more than halfway convinced *he* was going crazy. He and his house creature seemed to have made peace since Deb and Jeff figured out what the real trouble was.

"I'll ask you what I usually do," Deb said. "Not that I think you give me an honest answer most of the time.

Anyone get hurt at the old depot? Or have some kind of trouble I need to know about going in?"

Terri sat back with one hand on her chest, and an expression of wide-eyed shock.

"I cannot *believe* you accuse me in such a dreadful way, Deborah. Especially after the stressful and challenging week I've just had."

Deb got up and retrieved beers for herself, Jeff, and Wayne, pointedly ignoring Terri.

"Oh *no*, Theresa. Not you. You'd *never* leave things out to convince me to do what you want."

Terri shrugged and got a second beer for herself.

"Eh, depends on the circumstances. In this case, plenty of people got hurt at the old depot a long time ago, in a variety of unpleasant ways. But it's been calm for the last fifty years or so. Pretty much the usual with dumb kids messing around, like I did when my bad influence Powers cousins from Cincinnati came for a visit. The thing is you've been hanging out with Gina enough to know she's not exactly the overreacting type. And anyone who's tough enough to be a high school principal doesn't scare easily."

"But she's scared anyway," Jeff said.

Terri nodded. "Not even those crazy shadow things you found under the high school shook her up like this. She hasn't seen anything, but she's heard the sounds. Just to make sure I heard you right, Deb, you asked if you needed to know anything going in. Does that mean you *are* going in?"

Deb rolled her eyes, but for the first time she didn't have the heart to pretend, even to herself. The other weird cases Terri had brought her managed to completely rile up and wake up the insatiably curious part of her that drove her to get into PI work in the first place.

At this point, she already knew the computer business would be a side gig at best.

And she was happier than she wanted to admit about that.

"Yeah, I'm going in, and you know it. I'll have to read up on the history of the depot, get an idea what might be going on. I'm sure Auntie Zelda had books or something about it in the house somewhere."

Wayne surprised her by laughing.

"I can pretty much guarantee you she did." His curly silver hair glinted as he nodded. "She was always interviewing older folks before *we* turned into the older folks, making sure to keep up with the history. She had about fifteen years on me, but I never could understand how she had so much energy. Remembered every word, too, but I'd bet she wrote it all down."

"That she did," Terri said, slapping her thighs and getting up. "Remembered it, I mean. And I'm sure she made plenty of notes. And before you ask, Deb, I really am too wiped out for something like this, probably for at least a couple of days. Auntie Zelda had all that energy because she never had in-laws like mine. But I'd say if you give Gina a call, she'd be thrilled to get started whenever you're ready."

"You good to drive? You downed both of those in a big hurry." Deb tried not to imagine the sheriff getting hit with a DUI right in front of her house.

Especially since she'd given Terri the beer.

"Not driving," Terri said, her cheeks flushing enough to be noticeable. "That husband of mine drove me into town, trying to make up for exposing me to his family. Not that you offered me nearly enough to drink to have trouble walking myself back to the office."

She turned on her heel and left, her gait entirely solid and steady.

"You're going out there to the depot with Deb," Wayne said, leaning forward and smacking Jeff's knee. "Not 'cause she can't take real good care of herself, I know she can. You grew up hearing all about Estonoa's history from me and your papaw and granny and about everyone else, and that might help. I truly do wish I could go down there with you myself. But you don't want me slowing you down."

"You worked circles around both of us on this porch," Deb said. "Which I want to thank you for again if you'll let me make you dinner one night this week. If you want to walk down to one of the restaurants in town right now, I'm buying. Assuming any of them have time to feed us with the big festival coming up. I'll try to get in touch with Gina and see if she's ready for us to invade her space."

Wayne and Jeff smiled at each other in that natural, easy way Deb admired. She had a far more...traditional relationship with her own parents. Close enough, but never quite friendly.

"You're on," Jeff said, then surprised her by leaning over and kissing her cheek. "If Gina's willing tonight, I'll take Dad home after we eat. Then we'll see what we can't get into."

THE OLD ESTONOA train depot wasn't nearly as run-down as Deb remembered it, even by streetlights and the moon.

The wooden sides were freshly painted white, and the peaked roof and gracefully curved supports looked solid and clean as well. One black wrought-iron bench with wooden slats for the seat and back gleamed like new, while two others sat rusty and pitiful nearby, waiting for a similar restoration.

The wide wooden boards of the broad platform had partly been scrubbed clean, leaving some bright and others still dark with age and soot. From what Deb could see of the inside, the progress hadn't quite made it in there yet. The windows were mostly grimy except for a few that had just been replaced.

The mingled scents of paint and wood stain competed with the still-delicious aromas coming from at least two of the restaurants in town. Someone was baking overtime, while more onions were being called into service not too far away.

If Deb hadn't stuffed herself a little silly with excellent pizza earlier, she might have wandered off to beg a late-night snack from one of the people still cooking. *Very* late-night, since Gina had asked them to meet her at the unusual hour of two-thirty in the morning.

The night itself was still and quiet, with the breeze blowing through and sweeping away the day's heat. She hadn't been in town long enough to get used to that sharp day/night temperature contrast that made sleeping so delightful, especially compared to the unpleasantly long-lived evening heat in Atlanta.

The train tracks shone silver in the moonlight against the gray and white of huge gravels along the side. Trains still passed through Estonoa several times a day. But the often-riotous celebration that came with payday ended when they no longer made regular stops.

Only the wonderful old tradition of the annual Santa Train pulled into town these days, still distributing holiday gifts and joy as it had since the Great Depression.

"Looks like they're making amazing progress," Jeff said from beside her, peering into one of the new windows. "The town and the county both tried to tear this old place down a few times over the years. People fought that back, but no one stepped up to do something with the building until now."

They both turned at the crunch of someone walking across the fresh gravel in the parking lot. Gina Vanover, wearing jeans and a long-sleeved t-shirt rather than her normal sedate principal pantsuit or the more colorful versions she brought out for church on Sundays.

Her close-cut curly hair showed only a little darker than her skin in the faint light as she stepped in for a hug from Deb, then Jeff.

"Thank you both so much for coming down here," she said. "And so late, too. I keep telling myself you won't think I'm crazy for all this, especially since you've both seen plenty of the strangeness that goes on around here. Still, I feel more than a little bit foolish."

Deb shook her head. "You'd have to go a long way to top the eerie shadow critters under the high school. Or the eddy along the trail that quite reasonably freaked everyone out."

"Or the hillbilly fairies, or the unusual permanent resident out at the B&B." Jeff laughed, and Deb saw some of the tension go out of Gina's shoulders before he went on. "I hope you realize every single word that just came out of my mouth should keep you from being worried about anything you could possibly say."

Gina laughed as she dug a set of keys out of her pocket.

"You do have a point there. Okay, let's see what we can get figured out."

Strong hits of sawdust, paint, and coffee wafted out when Gina opened the door. The overhead lights weren't much brighter than outside, but Deb could see a much larger empty space inside than she expected.

Broad sheets of pale drop cloth covered the floor, and waist-high stacks of lumber lined one wall. Several cans of paint sat against another, with all kinds of brushes, rollers, and ladders waiting to get back to work. Deb recognized a big floor sander—looking like an oversized vacuum cleaner with an attitude problem—from work on her house in Atlanta years ago.

"We had everything delivered inside," Gina said, "mainly

because one of the board members was sure people would try to steal the lumber and tools and everything else. But no one has even pretended to bother us. At least not until the last little bit."

"What's been going on?" Deb said. "Terri mentioned noises, and things getting moved around?"

Gina walked over to a beautiful old tall-backed wooden bench, refinished to perfection and sitting opposite all the lumber. She nodded, brushed her fingers across the curved bottom of the bench, then sat heavily

"Yeah, that's part of what's been going on. I didn't tell the whole thing to the deputies because I didn't want... Well, you know how people can get. Especially when the high school principal starts sounding more than a little off-balance. Honestly, what it looks like to me is people are just wandering around messing with stuff. But I can't see why anyone would do that and not take anything, you know?"

Deb sat beside her, and they both watched Jeff walking slowly around the edges of the depot. The ticket room had a faint light on inside, showing the closet-sized space through what had to be a brand-new window with a decidedly old-fashioned round hole in the middle.

"Terri said something about footprints in the dust? And the doors getting unlocked?"

Gina waved one hand toward the floor.

"That's why we have the drop cloths in here now. The floor wasn't in bad shape at all, nothing like the platforms outside. But I kept coming in mornings and finding dust everywhere, and papers and debris that didn't make any sense at all. With footprints and streaks all through the whole thing."

She sighed, long and low. "As for the doors, if they weren't entirely manual deadbolts and regular old locks, I'd swear someone was using an app to mess with us. Workers getting locked in, or locked out depending on where they are. All of us have taken to making sure someone knows when we step into the restrooms, too. The idea of getting locked in here overnight when *whatever* it is happens makes my skin crawl."

Jeff stopped in front of them, hands on his hips.

"You think the trouble gets here overnight?" he said.

"I do," Gina said. "That's why I asked you two to come down here in the middle of the night, which I greatly appreciate. I hope you don't mind that I asked Annie to join us at the last minute."

As if Gina had summoned her, Deb looked up to see Annie Griffith walk through the door. Another wonderful new friend, Annie had been an amazing help to Deb with both the rather active cave under the high school and the odd disturbances along the trail in town.

Right now Annie's spill of red curls hung loose and free halfway down her back, though Deb expected her to wrangle it into place any second now. Rather than her usual flowing styles, she wore loose, charcoal gray pants and a red tank top that matched her hair perfectly.

"Am I too late?" Annie said, setting her purple backpack beside the door and trotting across the echoing space toward them. "I'm so sorry, it took me a while to get everything together."

Gina patted the bench beside her and smiled.

"You really think I'm going to fuss and holler about you actually showing up, at the last minute *and* in the middle of the damn night? All I'm doing is sitting here reflecting on the kinds of people I've been hanging out with lately. Mostly in a good way."

Annie leaned her head against Gina's shoulder for a second when she sat, then she did indeed twist her glorious hair into a tidier-than-usual knot.

"Thank the Goddess," Annie said. "I'd hate to get *this* group together and miss anything. What can I do to help?"

"You said something about a welcome?" Gina said, rubbing her arms. "Not that I'm convinced it's a good idea to welcome any more trouble than we've already got going on."

Annie popped up and almost skipped back over to her backpack.

"Sure thing! That's always a good place to start no matter what's going on."

Jeff rubbed his hands together exactly the same way he had as a geeky little kid, then sat beside Deb. When he slipped his arm around her shoulders, she managed not to smile at the careful smoothness of it all.

"I've known Annie as a passing acquaintance for years," he said. "But I've never gotten to see her at work."

Deb resisted the urge to scoot closer to him, or maybe put a hand on his thigh. The slow start to their friendship-with-possibilities had been a wonderful change of pace, and a great way to ease herself back into the idea of dating.

And she was also starting to think it was time to see if the rest of him was as easy on the eyes as his clothed body and face.

"Annie's a wonder," Gina said. "The kids love it every time she gives a talk, no matter whether it's gardening or spiritual traditions or anything else."

Deb started to ask if Annie needed help, then she shivered despite the perfectly comfortable warmth inside the depot, not to mention the comfort of Jeff's arm.

"Anyone else feel that? Like...I don't know, maybe a chilly breeze passing through?"

Jeff shook his head and moved closer to Deb. She got the feeling it was more for safety in numbers than affection, but she found she didn't mind either way.

"Not until you mentioned it. But I *am* hearing something. I think. Or maybe I'm feeling it?"

Gina stood, rubbing her hands against her thighs and looking around. Deb hadn't known her all that long, but she never would have imagined Gina's face so tight and drawn and uneasy.

"I'm feeling the breeze and the rumble," Gina said. "Can't *hear* much of anything besides my own fool heart hammering up a storm. This is the same time folks have been calling in complaining about the noise, but I've never been down here before when it happened."

Annie stopped in front of them, head tilted, backpack in hand.

"Wow, there's a *lot* going on here, huh?" She handed small crystals to everyone, and Deb recognized the same smoky gray one they'd used to figure out the trouble out along the trail.

"Just hold on to those crystals, I got them all charged up and ready to go over the last few days. Back out at Marlene's Eddy since Deb solved that mystery."

Deb started to protest that she'd hardly done that by herself, but she got a look at what Annie held in her hand and stopped. Jeff squeezed Deb's shoulders and got to his feet, holding his green-tinted crystal in one hand.

"Forgive me for being a bit ignorant about such things," he said. "But is that a water gun you've got there?"

Annie grinned and shook her bright pink plastic water gun.

"You bet it is. Remind me to tell you about the time I first used a much bigger on of these in a ritual unless Deb beats me to it. This one is loaded with rainwater I collected, then infused with those crystals, flower petals, and herbs from my garden. It sat out under the full moon, then I blessed it and had every clergy member in town do the same.

The water gun just makes it easier to distribute. But don't worry, this particular batch is made to welcome rather than banish."

Before Deb could say anything else, maybe about welcoming being a bad idea, she heard the rumble Jeff mentioned. And she felt it in the wood floor under her feet.

"Where did you find things, Gina?" Jeff walked around the room again, but this time more in the middle than around the edges. "All the stuff you mentioned earlier."

Gina held out her arms, and her rosy pink crystal flashed in the low light.

"Everywhere, really. The dust at least. I guess most of the old papers and junk were against the wall across from the ticket window. I hear there were luggage lockers there, but they disappeared a long time ago."

Deb turned, a snippet she'd read in her Auntie Zelda's notebooks flashing into her mind.

A sad story, something about...a young girl and her sweetheart, maybe?

And hadn't Jeff said something about people meeting up here earlier?

"Jeff, you mentioned this being a hot—"

The rumble turned itself up all at once, jumping from a distant tremble under Deb's feet to rattling her teeth.

"Hurry, come over here and join hands!" Annie shouted, standing in front of the wall across from the ticket window.

A couple of ladders leaned against the clean white surface, along with big push brooms and industrial-size trash cans. Deb tried to imagine a crush of people here over a hundred years ago, wearing suits and hats and long traveling dresses, returning home or setting out on a new adventure out in the world.

Jeff took her hand with the gray crystal, and she grasped Gina's chilly hand still holding the pink stone. Annie walked in a half-circle behind them, squeezing the trigger of her water gun what seemed like a hundred times a minute.

The hiss of Annie's extra-holy holy water arcing across the empty depot somehow cut through the roar that now rattled the ladders in front of them.

"If your spirit is unsettled," Annie called in a soothing voice, "let us bring you peace. Let us calm your soul, and lay your troubles to rest. Help us soothe your heart, and recover whatever has been lost to you. You're among friends here."

Annie walked back in front of the wall, and Deb saw she had the water gun set to spray a fine mist that lingered in the depot, adding to the already thick and substantial feel of the air.

It smelled of roses and thunder, fresh air and moonlight.

Annie stepped in between Jeff and Gina, tucking the water gun into her pocket before she grasped their hands, completing the circle.

"Set your heart and mind to welcoming a lost stranger," Annie said, raising her voice. "Maybe not home, because we can't know that yet. Welcome them to where they'll recover whatever they've been searching for."

Jeff squeezed Deb's hand, and his green eyes lit up as he opened his mouth. She had only a second to wonder how he was going to manage to speak above the roar that felt like it could shift the building off its foundation, and all of them loose from their own space and time.

Then all four of them focused on the mist still hanging in front of the wall where the luggage lockers once stood.

Where a shadowy figure now drifted, slowly resolving into the shape of an achingly beautiful young woman.

She wore a dark bonnet that framed her heart-shaped face, and a full, floor-length dress that buttoned at her delicate neck and wrists. Deb couldn't see any sort of luggage or anything else forming around her, but the woman seemed to be searching for something.

Turning from one side to the other, hands clasped at her waist. Glancing over her shoulder toward the ticket window, then the door.

But her dark, worried eyes kept returning to the drop-cloth-covered floor under one of the ladders.

Deb's heart thumped inside her chest, and both Jeff and Gina squeezed her hands hard enough that the sharp edges of the crystals verged on painful. And it was everything Deb could do to keep from pulling her hands away so she could cover her ears against the horrible rumble that grew ever louder.

"Welcome, traveler," Annie said with a soft smile, her voice cutting through the furious noise. "Let us help you if we can."

The woman spun, her dress flaring out around her legs, hands flying up to cover her mouth.

A metallic shriek like a jagged blow to Deb's skull rose up, and she finally realized what she was hearing.

An enormous train, surely larger than had ever passed through Estonoa or anywhere else in the world.

A train that had just hit the brakes, hard.

"We won't hurt you, child," Gina said. "All of us are here to ease your soul."

The woman slowly lowered her hands, staring wild-eyed at all of them.

"Louise?" Jeff said, leaning forward. "Louise Traseda?"

The spectral woman's gaze focused laser-sharp on him, and Deb almost drew him back and away.

Every bit of the noise stopped at once.

Leaving Deb's ears ringing in the deep silence, until the ghostly woman spoke.

"Who is it that knows my name in this strange place?"

The words were whispery but perfectly clear, with an accent that hadn't come from anywhere in these mountains.

"My name is Annie. And this is Gina, and Deb, and Jeff. Are you searching for something, Louise?"

Deb's mind cleared in a flash at the word *searching*, and she remembered everything written in her Auntie Zelda's neat script.

Louise drew herself up and lifted her chin, but she didn't look disdainful or dismissive.

She looked determined.

And hopeful.

"My companion was to meet me here three days ago, on the overnight train from Hidden Springs. I daresay there's been a problem of some kind, but I can't imagine she wouldn't have gotten word to me somehow. We arranged a means of communicating, you see, in case one of us should be delayed."

Jeff nodded. "You had a hiding place. Where you could leave notes, or have someone deliver them for you."

Louise covered her mouth with one fine-boned hand for a second.

"Have you heard from her, sir? Or do you perhaps have something written in her own hand?"

"I wish we did, Louise," he said. "Can you tell us where you hid things?"

This time Louise buried her face in her hands, muffling her words, but not the pain and confusion behind them.

"I cannot *remember*! My mind has gone unreliable, and at the worst possible time it could have."

Deb's heart twisted instead of pounding now, and for the first time in her life, she wished she didn't remember her Auntie Zelda's words.

"We may still be able to help you," she said. "Gina, you

said you found old papers with all the dust. Where were those?"

Gina let go of Deb's and Annie's hands and stepped forward, into the middle of the circle. Louise hadn't yet looked up, and the heartbreaking sound of her crying filled the room.

"All along the base of the wall," she said. "Almost exactly where Louise is standing."

"Where the old lockers were," Deb said. "Annie, do you think you can aim your holy water or welcoming water along there again? Maybe more toward the floor?"

Annie stepped forward at once, pausing beside Louise.

"We'll do our best for you, and help your soul find rest."

Then she brought the squirt gun up again, squeezing madly toward the base of the wall.

The mist filled the air as it had before, along with the flowery, thundery scent.

But this time, a faint pink glow rose up all around them, before it concentrated into a spot just above the ground cloth.

"There!" Jeff nearly leapt toward the glow, moving the ladder and rolling the drop cloth out of the way. He knelt and reached for the floor before he looked over his shoulder at Gina. "Is it okay with you if I see what I can find under here?"

Gina laughed under her breath: the sound strange against Louise's soft, agonized cries.

"Please do, and let me help if I can."

Jeff thumped the floorboards all along the wall, and Deb wasn't surprised to hear one of them give a hollow thud. She grabbed a hammer from a little pile of tools and knelt beside him.

Between his fingers and the claw end of the hammer, they pried the loose floorboard up with no trouble at all.

Deb pulled out her phone and thumbed the flashlight on, shining it down into a dusty space only a few inches deep.

"It's an envelope," Jeff whispered. He reached down and carefully grasped it between his thumb and finger. A thick layer of dust shifted and fell with the movement. "Nothing but L T written on the outside."

"Louise?" Annie said from behind them. "I think this must be for you."

Louise hesitated for a second, and her shoulders rose and fell. Then she lowered her hands and slowly walked over. Deb wondered whether she'd be able to physically take the envelope, but Louise answered that question with her next words.

"Could you please read it to me, kind sir? I'm afraid I've been having trouble with my eyes as well as my mind as of late."

Deb spoke in a low voice as Jeff carefully opened the envelope.

"Louise, have you been feeling ill lately? With a dreadful high fever, and red spots on your skin?"

Louise covered one forearm with her other hand even though her dress went all the way down to her wrists.

"I have fevered and had a most distressing rash, but it was not the smallpox. I'm quite sure of it. That scourge has never made it all the way to these mountains, and I can assure you we have no reason to believe it *ever* will."

Deb stood just as Jeff whispered.

"But it did. Not many cases, and not for long. It's one of Estonoa's better-kept secrets."

"Not as well-kept as what I think you're about to read," Deb said.

Louise folded her hands together at her waist again, staring at Jeff with hope so plain and true that Deb had to look away.

"My dearest," he read. "I'm afraid I've been called away, back home to Philadelphia, much sooner than expected. I shall leave a ticket for your passage. You only need show it to the agent, and he'll help get you on your way to me at last. Yours in loving anticipation, Eva."

When Deb looked back at Louise, her face had gone from hopeful to radiant.

"Is it truly so?" she said in a breathy voice. "She made passage for me, and she awaits?"

Jeff unfolded another sheet of fragile paper, revealing a hand-printed ticket inside.

"I have it right here," he said, his voice trembling. "A ticket to Philadelphia, and directions to a house there written on this paper. In case she's unable to meet you, it says."

Louise raised her clasped hands under her chin with a smile as bright as a cloudless summer day.

"Then I must regretfully take my leave of you, with my eternal gratitude for your help. I'll be certain to remember you to Eva upon my arrival."

Without another word or backward glance, Louise walked toward the ticket window.

While they watched, Deb would have sworn the light inside that tiny little room grew brighter, and the shadowy shape of a man moved within.

Louise went to the door, turned and held up one hand in farewell, then passed through as easily as the mist still floating all around them.

The silence in the depot was complete.

"She had smallpox," Jeff finally said. "Probably delirious from the fever. I'd never heard that part of the story. I only knew her name, and that she supposedly had some kind of heartbreak all those years ago before she died young."

"She's gone now," Annie said. "Can't you feel the difference? She finally caught her train. And she's *happy.*"

Gina put an arm around Annie, and Deb saw her dash away tears.

"I feel it," Gina said. "Something shifted, all around us. For the better."

"Auntie Zelda's notes mentioned smallpox," Deb said, "and how one woman raved with fever for several days before she recovered. She kept saying she had to find it, to keep searching. Over and over again. But no one could ever figure out what she meant. And she did die, not long after, even though no one could figure out the cause."

Jeff put his arm around her again, and Deb leaned against him.

"I'd say she died of a broken heart," he said. "Maybe we just helped mend it."

The spell broken, all four of them gathered their things and got ready to leave.

Remembering ghostly Louise's radiant face as she departed Estonoa at long last, Deb's mind finally caught up to the suggestion her heart had been making for a good long while now.

She caught Jeff's hand before he got to the door, pulled him close, and kissed him good and long and proper. This time the tingles and fireworks gave way to full-body explosions.

"I think it's time I got as bold and daring as Louise was," she whispered when they drew apart. "How'd you like to come back home with me tonight?"

He grinned and kissed her until both of them had to come up for air.

"I thought you'd never ask. And the answer is let's get there fast as we can."

Gina's expertly cleared throat somehow echoed all the way from the outside of the depot to the inside, no doubt a trick she routinely employed to get rowdy, hormone-addled high school kids' attention. She stood in the doorway, arms crossed, one foot tapping.

"If you two have *quite* finished with your rather bold public display of affection, I'd like to lock up so we can all go home for the night? I would have thought you were old enough to know where to take that kind of extracurricular activity."

Annie's curl-adorned head peeked over Gina's shoulder.

"Can't you *see*, Gina? It's the last echo of Louise and her lover, meeting each other on that train platform in Philadelphia after all this time. I say we're blessed to witness the circle of love play out right in front of us like this."

Gina snorted and shook her head, then stepped back and held the door open for Deb and Jeff to pass through.

"I don't know about *blessed*," Gina said. "I do know I'll be glad to get home to my own bed and a good night's sleep. If anyone else decides to make a different choice in their own bedroom, that's no business of mine."

She smiled at Deb before she turned to lock the train depot door.

"I hope you'll both forgive me for saying it's about damn time."

Jeff smiled at Deb, and she wondered if some of Annie's holy welcome water managed to follow them out the door.

All at once she saw the scrawny little boy, the gangly teenager, the comfortably mature and confident man.

All three of them watching her with that same expression of joy and acceptance.

Maybe she'd been the one not paying attention all along.

"Not a thing to forgive as far as I can tell," she said, slipping her arm around Jeff's waist, and returning his smile when he put his around her shoulders. "Truth is it's past damn time. Come on, handsome. Let's see if we can figure out what comes next."

ABOUT KARI

The daughter, granddaughter, and great-granddaughter of coal miners, Kari Kilgore's wanderlust and imagination lead her all over the world on grand adventures. Her heart and family bring her home to her native Appalachian Mountains of Virginia. From that solid base, she and her husband Jason A. Adams bring those adventures to life in fiction.

Kari writes mystery, fantasy, science fiction, romance, and contemporary fiction, and she's happiest when she surprises herself. She lives at the end of a long dirt road in the middle of the woods with Jason, various house critters, and wildlife they're better off not knowing more about.

The Confidential Adventure Club

For Kari's exclusive free After The End stories and deleted scenes, discounts, early pre-sale releases, adorable pet photos, and a whole lot more not available anywhere else, swing by
www.ConfidentialAdventureClub.com.

Hope to see you there!

www.KariKilgore.com
www.SpiralPublishing.net

ALSO BY KARI KILGORE

I hope you enjoyed reading the stories in *Investigations Beyond Belief* as much as I enjoyed writing them.

You'll find more mystery and crime short stories, novellas, and novels at www.KariKilgore.com/Mystery. If you love tales of fantasy, be sure to check out www.KariKilgore.com/Fantasy.

For more adventures from the Appalachian Mountains of Virginia and around the region, and in many genres, head over to www.KariKilgore.com/TalesFromAppalachia.

Be the first to know about release dates and check out more of my fiction, including almost every genre, at www.KariKilgore.com.

The Confidential Adventure Club

Want more fiction from Kari, including stories, discounts, and box sets not available anywhere else? Want to hear about locations, research, and other cool things that inspired this story and beyond? Want all that and adorable pet photos, too?

Join The Confidential Adventure Club and get a thank you gift of a free short story and a whole lot more. www.ConfidentialAdventureClub.com.

Hope to see you there!

The Storms of Future Past Series:

Dreaming the Storm

Joining the Storm

Into the Storm

Fighting the Storm

Sensing the Storm: A Storms of Future Past Prequel

Storms of the Heart: A Storms of Future Past Romance

Storms of Future Past Books One through Four Collection

The Odd Society:

Independent by Means of Magic

Protected by Means of Magic

The Voices through Time Series:

Songs in the Mountain

Secrets in the Land

Walking the Ghosts: A Voices through Time Novella

Dispatches from the Galaxy Stories:

Restricted Species

The Becalmed

The Garbage Belt

Plurapod Pathogen

The Changes Cascade

Novels:

Until Death

The Dream Thief

Hand Me Downs

Protecting Her Own

Novellas:

Legacy of the Land

In the Pines

DNA Never Lies

The Box of Possibilities

Collections:

Fantastic Women: A Dark Fantasy Novella Trio

Fantastic Shorts: Volume 1

Near Future Forward (with Jason A. Adams)

Fantastic Shorts: Volume 2

Partners in Romance (with Jason A. Adams)

Dispatches from the Galaxy: A Space Opera Novella Trio

Fantastic Shorts: Volume 3

Escape into Romance: A Collection of Sweet Beginnings

Stepping Out of Reality: Short Spells of Appalachian Magic

Facing Down Extraordinary: A Series of Ordinary Heroes

Hacking Cybercrime: Dana Sanderson Short Mysteries

Shadows Mountain Deep (with Jason A. Adams)

ADDITIONAL COPYRIGHT INFORMATION